Light of the Black Sails

Written and Illustrated By
Brandy Collins

Author: Brandy Collins
Editors: Amy Collins, Charlie Collins, Danielle LaPat, Brandon Collins, Mary Collins, Cody Collins
Cover Design: Brandy Collins, Charlie Collins
Cover Illustration: Brandy Collins
Interior Illustrations: Brandy Collins

Printed in the United States of America

Published by Brandy Collins

This book is dedicated to Mimi

The Parts of a Ship

9

Prologue

A young girl stood on the deck of the frigate, *Princess Anne*, fumbling with a spyglass. It was much too big for her, but she clumsily raised it to her eye to peer through it anyway. Scanning the horizon with the awkward instrument, a shape caught her eye. Sails. A ship. She watched for a few moments.

The hull was flawless and defined, slicing through the gentle waves effortlessly. Three rows of oars impelled the vessel forward in perfect harmony. The galleon turned sharply, the sails furrowed, and the oars began to thrust faster into the swelling waves.

"Papa," the girl called from across the deck as she leaned over the railing. She kept her eyes on the galleon. Her father strode on long legs over to his daughter.

"Aye, Tip?"

"There are sails over there, Papa, and they are following our ship." The girl pointed with a small, slender finger out over the sea.

The man peered out over the choppy waters, just able to make out the tips of the high masts of the sleek vessel.

"It is a ship, but I don't think they are following us…" the man was puzzled. The vessel wasn't on the charts.

"They're black sails, Papa."

The man took the spyglass from her and looked out through the lens. His throat tightened. His worst fear was definitely pursuing his ship. The galleon came quickly into view; the black sails and hull were unmistakable as the ship knifed through the waves. The man knew they couldn't outrun the galleon, for it was already gaining behind them.

"All hands on deck! Ready the long guns!" called the captain. By now, the crew was rushing around, preparing for the attack that swiftly followed. Four cannons firing from the black galleon at the frigate boomed and caused cannonballs to soar through the air towards their target. Two struck low, the other two struck high. The high balls hit the mast and sails. The other two were low, splintering into the hull of the ship. The man held his daughter close to him as he fought through the smoke and chaos. The black galleon pulled up close to the navy ship, not even lowering the gangplank before the black-clad pirates started swarming aboard. The man had climbed down to the first deck below, as safe as he could think of for the moment, and shoved his daughter behind some boxes. Stacking the cargo around the girl like a wall, he whispered to her.

“Don’t come out unless you can't hear anything or you think the ship is sinking. I'll come back if I can. Stay quiet,”

“But…”

“Hush,” he quieted, “I love you very much, my Tip.” He kissed her forehead and then he was gone. The girl huddled in the corner as she listened to the pirates swarm into the hold. Tears flowed down her cheeks, but she didn’t make a sound. Minutes passed, feeling like hours to her. She became aware of more pirates coming down below deck, hooting and snarling like ravaged animals.

Suddenly, the pile of boxes began to be pulled down. Tip crawled closer into the corner, hoping she wouldn't be found. A box fell onto her, and she gave a small cry as the corner of it hit her ribs.

"What's this?" a harsh, callous voice crowed. Beefy hands grabbed Tip by her waist and hauled her up. She fought back helplessly in vain, beating her small white hands on the barrel chest of her captor. The man laughed, his tattoos of serpents on his upper arms grinning venomously at her, and he withdrew a small dagger. She screamed and struggled to escape the evil man's grip. He slid the knife closer to her throat.

Another tar-covered hand came between them, placing a thick finger on the blade of the knife. Tip's tattooed captor looked up at the other man, an irritated look on his portly face.

"What is it?" he snarled.

"Give her to the captain. He may want her, the small thing," Tip's rescuer said. He eyed the girl. He had blood running down his right arm and dripping red from his silver cutlass blade. Tip could not tell if the blood was his or not.

The tattooed man grunted, then whipped the girl around. He snatched up a rope that was lying on the wooden floor and yanked the knots tight as he bound Tip's wrists together. She whimpered. The rope cut into her wrists and bruised her tender skin. He then shoved her ahead of him, forcing her to walk towards the ladder that went to the upper decks. Both men laughed cruelly when she tripped on a rung and hit her jaw sharply on the wood. Tears sprang into her green eyes. She blinked them back, willing herself to not cry. Roughly, she was hefted up by the tattooed pirate and slung over his burly shoulder.

Coughing from the smoke, Tip came up on deck upon the pirate. Instantly, she knew that they had lost the battle. Men from her ship's crew lay bloody and disfigured on the decks in the smoky haze. She shut her eyes tight, but she could still see the bodies in her mind.

The tattooed pirate bounded over the deck and leaped over to the black-sailed ship. She gasped as she saw water, then pure, pitch-black wood. Her teeth chattered together as the man landed on the deck of the black galleon. He set her down forcefully and she faced a taller, darker figure.

The man in front of her was tall and lean, clothed in black boots, black trousers, a bright red belt, a white cotton shirt, and a long, black coat. His dark, pointed beard was waxed and trimmed neatly, and his dark hair was parted smartly and tied back in a short braid with a black ribbon. His eyes were stormy grey, and they stared into Tip's green eyes.

"A girl," he said softly, coming closer to her. She felt sick and tense. The man laughed evilly, and then reached out to stroke her cheek. She flinched. His hands were ice cold. "How old are you?"

"E-e-eleven, sir," she said timidly.

"So young," he said. His hand reached into his belt and slowly pulled out a pistol. She swallowed. He was going to kill her. Tip looked around desperately for her father, for anyone familiar. Then she spotted him, blindfolded and gagged, along with several of the crew. He knew she was there, even though he couldn't see her. He knew that she was going to be shot with that weapon, and he couldn't do anything to protect her. Tip bit her lip and began to cry. She tried to stop, wanting to be brave, but she couldn't. She was too terrified. Her hands and knees shook terribly.

"Little girl," he said softly, holding the gun up to the light, admiring it. "I'm not going to kill you. I'm not even going to hurt you,"

Tip shuddered. What was he talking about? What was he going to do?

"I have chosen you to be my living witness to my destruction." he swept his arm in a circle and pointed from the sinking sloop with all the dead bodies on it to the disarmed prisoners on the black deck. "Take it in, young one, remember,"

Tip looked where he gestured, trembling and confused. Why was she supposed to remember this horrible scene?

"Run to your sinking ship," the man said. He cut the ropes that bound her thin wrists, and when she didn't move, he yelled, "Go!"

Tip turned and ran over the rickety plank and stumbled onto the bloody deck. The plank was pulled back onto the ship immediately. The man laughed vociferously as he fired the pistol three times into the air; the black sails sped away, leaving the girl alone on the silent, sinking vessel.

Chapter One

Five Years Later...

The ships lined the harbor as diamonds on a necklace, flying their various flags. The sun shone brightly in the cloudless sky and a springtime breeze blew through the streets of the village. Merchants lined the busy streets, calling out to potential customers to purchase their wares. Most of the people walking through the streets were sailors, pirates, merchants, or voyagers, all coming into port to stock their vessels after a long and hard winter.

Wilam Eugene dodged through the harbor streets, weaving in and out between merchants. His tall, lanky frame was clad in sailors' garb; a cotton shirt, black boots, and worn trousers. He pushed wavy light-brown hair from his hazel eyes and blended into the crowd. Occasionally, he would crash into a stand, causing merchandise to spill out onto the road. The street vendors weren't pleased to have the young man interrupt their hawking and cursed at him as he went by. He chuckled to himself. What the merchants didn't know was that the sandy-haired teenager was quietly slipping some merchandise into his pockets as he helped to pick up what he had knocked over.

"You there! Boy!" A fat merchant called, pointing his finger at Wilam. Wilam didn't wait to see what the man wanted. He ducked his head and merged between the swarms of people to be mixed in with the masses. Wilam refused to get caught for his thievery his first day in port.

Stepping over a crate of chickens, Wilam started searching for the tavern where he and Jack had arranged to meet. Jack Cadett was Wilam's fellow crewmate on the *Farrow* and his closest friend on the ship. Jack was the one who had invited Wilam to join the crew, with permission from the captain of the *Farrow*, Captain John Halkins. Jack was nineteen. Wilam, however, was the youngest member of the crew now at seventeen years of age.

Locating the tavern, Wilam stepped through the entrance, relieved to be out of the throngs of sweaty bodies. The tavern was spacious and surprisingly clean with a number of tables and several booths; half of which were presently occupied. Wilam located Jack in the corner booth and strolled over to him. Sliding into the chair next to his friend, Wilam proceeded to empty his pockets of his stolen goods. Two cakes, a blue woolen scarf, a small paring knife, an apple, a whittled comb, and a metal ring made from a blacksmith's nail.

Jack, slouching in his chair with his arms crossed, raised an eyebrow.

"You've been busy, I see," he remarked. Wilam's hazel brown eyes flashed as he grinned. He swept everything but the comb into his small sack he kept at his belt. "What are you going to do with that rubbish?"

Wilam pretended to act insulted.

"Rubbish indeed, my dear sir!" he exclaimed with an exaggerated, high-society accent, picking up his comb and running it through his long, sandy brown hair, "This fine comb is molded of the purest silver, and engraved with the works of a master silversmith who crafts ornaments for the grand ladies of the palaces!"

"It's birch wood, Will," Jack stated, a smile perking on his lips. Will just raised his eyebrows in a knowing way and continued to groom his hair with his dear comb. Jack sighed. "Why do you keep stealing?"

“Habit, I guess. It was my only way to eat for several years,”

“But you get paid your lay like the rest of the crew of the *Farrow*. Isn’t that good enough?”

“Jack,” Wilam sighed, exasperated. “I want to have fun while we are in port, so don’t spoil it for me. Not today.”

Jack shrugged, and then nodded. Abruptly, he reeled around as a loud clatter was heard from the tavern kitchen. Several tin plates had crashed and scattered on the floor. Clutching the arm of one of the tavern girls, the large greasy cook began yelling at her, calling her worthless as he dragged her out of the kitchen. He slapped her hard across her face. With her other hand, she touched the red mark on her cheek from the clout she had received. With a final harsh rebuke, he thrust her away forcibly so that she stumbled into a table; the tavern keeper turned back to his kitchen in a huff to pick up the tin dishes. The girl pushed her fingers through her hair, and then saw the two sailors at the booth; she took a deep breath and walked towards them. She appeared at the table, an apron around her waist and a tired, forced smile on her pretty face. Her dark hair was wrapped around her head, keeping it out of her way while she served the customers.

"What will you be having this afternoon?" she asked. Jack ordered meat and potatoes and Wilam ordered the same. The girl nodded and then went to get their food.

"So, Will," Jack said, resting his elbows on the table, "I've been asking around, gathering information from the locals about the ships. There have been five ships now that have gone missing. Gone. Disappeared. Without a trace."

"And?" Will wrinkled his eyebrows together. His tongue stuck out in concentration as he tied his long hair back. It came to about shoulder-length. "Does anyone know what happened?"

Jack shook his head, his black hair falling into his cerulean eyes.

"Not really. This has been going on for about five years now, according to Captain Halkins. Ships just disappear without a trace around here." Jack suddenly leaned forward, "They say there is a pirate convoy that's doing it."

The girl came back to the table with two steaming plates of food, setting them on the table in front of the two young men.

“There you are,” she said. “I'll be back with your drinks. Whiskey, ale, milk, or water?”

“Is the whiskey good?” Jack asked her. She shrugged.

“I don’t drink it, though I have had no complaints,”

“I'll take it,” Jack said. The girl turned to Wilam.

“And you, sir?”

“I'll have the same.” Wilam answered, and then said, “Thank you.”

She suddenly smiled. Wilam liked the sparkle that flared in her green eyes; though he noticed the red mark still dwelled on her pale cheek. “In all my time working here, no one has ever thanked me before. Thank you for thanking me!” she left, and Wilam watched her for a moment with curiosity before turning back to Jack.

“So what do you mean, a pirate convoy?” Wilam asked, continuing the conversation as he dug into his meal.

"Halkins believes the pirates are in a convoy. A fleet. People say the ships have black sails, and overtake a ship in an area. Halkins wants to find these pirates and also find out what happened to the ships," Jack said. The young men looked up to see the tavern girl again, this time with drinks in hand. She set the drinks down in front of them, pausing.

"You said the name Halkins?" she asked, rather reticently. Jack nodded. "As in…Captain John Halkins?"

"Aye, miss," Jack said, turning to her. "He is our captain, captain on the *Farrow*. Do you know him?"

"Oh…I…I…No…I thought you said something about…black sails," she murmured, "You say he wants to find the ship? The black sailed ship?"

"Aye, so that's what he tells us. He wants to find the pirates that did it." Jack said. "What do you know about it?"

The girl stammered, fumbling for words. "I…I don't know…" Suddenly, she turned away and left the table. Jack shrugged, facing Wilam once again

"What stories do they have about these black-sailed pirate convoy ships?" Wilam asked Jack.

“One shipwreck from the navy was found near here with one survivor on board. He had drifted in close enough to be seen and found by a local fisherman. The man was rather old and crazy, having been alone for nearly six weeks. He said he had to eat the rotting corpses on the destroyed ship to survive. Nonetheless, when he was brought to the fisherman’s village, that’s near this town, and questioned about what had happened, he muttered some nonsense.” Jack paused, taking a few bites out of his food. Wilam waited for him to continue. “One thing they understood, though, was *black sails*.”

Chapter Two

That night brought in a storm. Rain thundered against the windows of the captain's quarters in the stern of the *Farrow.* Captain John Halkins sighed as he sat at his desk, looking at the charts in front of him. Odd shadows were cast on the wooden walls of the ship by the swaying oil lantern as the ship bobbed in the harbor waters. He pushed back the papers, rested his elbows on the desk, and rubbed his sleep-deprived blue eyes with his calloused hands. His dark, grizzled hair fell over his forehead as he leaned back in his chair and stroked his graying beard.

"What am I doing?" he mumbled. He began to organize his charts and maps to put them away when, suddenly, someone rapped on his door. Halkins frowned for a moment. Nearly all of his crew went on shore from the storm, and no one would dare knock at this hour.

"Aye?" he growled, not willing to leave his seat for an insensitive crewman.

"Captain John Halkins?" a female voice called. He sat up immediately. What woman would come to his ship, and know his name? He didn't know any women…not anymore.

"Come in," he said, not as harsh this time. The door opened and a figure in a dark cloak stepped in. When the person removed the hood, she stepped in front of the captain's desk. She was young, about sixteen, the captain observed, and not quite a full-grown woman. She stood tall. Confident.

"My name is Kathryn Thatcher. My father knew you,"

"Who, may I ask, is your father?" Halkins leaned back in his chair.

"Thomas Thatcher, sir," she answered.

"Ah, aye. I recall that old chap. Good man. Sailed with him years ago." Halkins nodded. "How is the man? Haven't seen him in a few years,"

"That is the thing, sir," Kathryn said, "This morning, in the tavern I work for, two of your crewmen came in. As I was serving them their food, I overheard them talking about your undertaking a mission to find a black-sailed ship," she paused.

"Go on," Halkins muttered, his thick eyebrows knitted together with curiosity. Why would this girl be interested in his seemingly ridiculous mission?

"Five years ago, my father and I were passengers on the frigate, *Princess Anne*, going to the city of New Harbour. A pitch-black galleon with three rows of oars overtook us, and rapidly came parallel to us in a matter of moments. I remember not the name of this black ship. When they attacked, my father was taken prisoner. The captain was all dressed in black and red, and he put me on the sinking ship after they looted it, saying: 'I have chosen you to be my living witness to my destruction.'" The girl said, her strong voice shaking slightly. The captain leaned forward with renewed interest.

"Fascinating!" he said, his eyes lighting up. "This is amazing, Miss Thatcher," he found a pen and a blank parchment. "Describe the ship and the captain again,"

"Well," she began, and then had an idea. "Perhaps I could draw it, instead, sir?"

Halkins handed over the material without a word. Raising an eyebrow, he observed the girl. She focused on her sketching, carefully depicting the gentle curve of the hull. Her dark, brunette hair was plaited in a single braid over her shoulder, coming nearly to her waist. Her heart-shaped face was a golden brown hue, beautifully contrasted by bright green eyes and perfect, full pink lips. She was a stunning young woman, Halkins thought. He felt a sudden pain in his chest for the girl who had lived without a father for five years. His heart ached for the man who had been her protector, her provider, and then was snatched away…away from his young daughter with no way to know what happened to her. If he was still alive, that is.

"How did you escape from the ship after the attack?" he asked finally.

"I escaped by rowing on a life boat to this harbor since it was so near,"

"Do you have family…other than your father?" he asked quietly. Kathryn blinked, and then continued her sketching.

"No," Kathryn said sadly, and then whispered, "I don't have any family other than my father. My mother died when I was a baby, and I had no brothers or sisters. When I came to the harbor, I did what work I could to earn a living and buy my food. No one wanted to care for a poor orphan…I would have been just another mouth to feed. So, I worked and made my home wherever I could find work. No one, except for you, knows what really happened to me."

Halkins was silent. He remembered, painfully, the loss of his own child so many years ago. He searched desperately for something to say to fill the deafening silence.

"Why do you tell me this?"

She hesitated for a moment before adding: "I've always been afraid to tell anyone. When I heard your crewmembers in the tavern today, I knew you could help me,"

"Me? How?" John Halkins huffed. She slid the finished diagram over to the man, a nearly perfect depiction of the black ship and the evil captain's face.

"I'm going with you on your ship to find my father."

Chapter Three

Sunday,

I have been on the Farrow for four days now. It is remarkable that I am finally on my way to finding Papa. Captain John Halkins was very hesitant to let me on the ship due to some of the sailors being superstitious of women on their ship. I showed them how versatile I was in the kitchen and cooked them the best food they've had in a while. They surrendered. I have my own quarters in the hold made from a wall of cargo. Barrels and the like. There are rats. I don't mind it, though. At least it is away from the men. I'm afraid I do not trust most of them. Oh, how I miss Papa. I fear he may not be alive. I shall only hope that this is not the case. ~Kathryn B. Thatcher

Kathryn closed her notebook and placed it in the pocket of her worn, green dress along with her bit of charcoal. She leaned out at the bowsprit, looking out over the glassy ocean water, smiling as drops of salty seawater sprayed her face. She loved being on the ocean, but it brought back the memories of her and her father, passengers aboard the *Princess Anne*. She smiled again, sadly this time. She closed her eyes, feeling the warm sun on her face. A hooting and hollering brought her back to reality, and she looked up to see Jack and Wilam patching the sails up on the foremast. Barefoot and shirtless, they joked around, stitching for a moment and then attempting to shove the other off the mast yard the next. Jack suddenly burst out laughing as he succeeded in pushing Wilam off-balance.

Kathryn's eyebrows shot up with surprise as Wilam merely flipped upside-down on the mast yard, his legs wrapped tightly around the pole that supported the sail as he suspended ten meters above the deck. He continued patching the sail below him nonchalantly, a clever smirk on his handsome face.

On the back of Wilam's left shoulder, Kathryn noticed an odd tattoo. It was a ship…a galleon. It struck her as peculiar for some reason.

Wilam dared a glance from his high perch at the young lady on the deck below him. She was watching intently, a smile playing on her lips. He winked at her.

She turned back to the waves, her long, dark hair gently waving in the breeze.

Kathryn laughed into the ocean, not willing to give Wilam the satisfaction of her amusement. If she wasn't careful, she could find herself smitten with the handsome young sailor. However, she wondered about his tattoo…

Pulling the coarse thread taut and snapping it with his teeth, Wilam swung up, righting himself on the mast yard next to Jack. He leaned against the mast and dangled his bare foot over the edge. He crossed his arms athwart his chest, still observing Kathryn Thatcher.

"What do you think about her?" he asked Jack as his friend pulled on his shirt.

"Miss Thatcher?" Jack questioned, raising a dark eyebrow curiously.

"Aye," Wilam said. Jack shrugged.

"A beautiful girl. She isn't an ordinary female," Jack commented, glancing also at the girl. "She seems like she enjoys the sea, and hasn't gotten the least bit seasick like that old, pompous Lady Birch who traveled with us that one time. Remember?"

"Aye," Wilam laughed at the memory, "What a grouchy old hag she was! 'These quarters are atrocious!

Oh, my poor hair! Do you not understand the work it is to keep a wig so powdered? Good heavens! Is that a *rat*?'"

Jack and Wilam laughed together.

"Miss Thatcher's hands aren't soft, either," Jack continued, "She knows a hard day's work,"

"How do you know if her hands are soft or not?" Wilam asked, a little too quickly, sitting upright and staring at Jack. Jack laughed at the stiff look on Wilam's face, realizing what he was thinking.

"I can *see* the calluses, Will. I don't need to hold her hand," Jack said lightheartedly. Wilam let out a breath he didn't realize he was holding, and leaned back once more against the mast. He looked down again at the girl on the deck, content to just watch her. He felt as if he could gaze at her for hours.

As if sensing that he was staring at her, Kathryn looked up at Wilam, her green eyes shimmering in perfect hue to her simple dress. Wilam nodded in exaggerated civility, dobbing an invisible top hat to her. She smiled kindly, but then turned away once again. She normally tried to steer clear of him. Kathryn leaned against the balustrade of the deck, removing her journal once again.

Same day,

I feel like a rather foolish girl, writing this about a young man on the Farrow, *because I always thought of myself as sensible and cautious. A young man on the ship seems to be quite taken with me, and I find myself thinking of him as rather attractive. His name, I have discovered, is Wilam Eugene. His name is said: Will-lum, instead of the more common Will-li-um. I do not think Eugene is his surname, though. I wonder about his odd tattoo on his left shoulder. What is so strange about it? No matter... I shall continue to be cautious around him and not encourage him. I must remember that I am the only woman on the ship. ~KBT*

Kathryn closed her notebook, again slipping it into her dress pocket. Wilam was handsome, she thought, but Papa would never approve. Satisfied with that final reflection, she stood up straight, squared her shoulders, and strode off to the galley where she would help prepare the evening meal.

Chapter Four

Wilam coughed as a brawny hand planted itself in the middle of his chest and slammed him into the wooden wall. The hand belonged to a huge, bald man. He growled, pulling his lips back in a sneer.

"What did you just say?" the man snarled, his fingers digging into Wilam's chest.

"I said nay," Wilam wheezed, "I won't rebel against the captain, George,"

"With me as captain, we'll be rich, Will, with action, adventure...piracy," George glared at the boy. "You're young, boy. You'll make a good buccaneer and be a terror of the seas. You're out of the ordinary, Wilam Eugene. I see something in you,"

"No," Wilam gasped.

A clout to the jaw sent Wilam to the ground. George stood above him, his bald, shiny head red with rage. He bent over and picked Wilam up by the front of his shirt.

“If you know what’s good for you, Will, you’ll think about how you speak to me,” George said, “I'm offering you an opportunity of a lifetime!”

Wilam hesitated, his mouth open. He had always dreamed of becoming rich and powerful ever since he was a little boy. He snapped his mouth shut and licked his dry lips.

“You may even get to be captain of your own ship,” George whispered, softly this time.

“How?” Wilam asked, “If I mutiny with you, and we do defeat the captain, wouldn’t you be the captain on this ship…only?” He felt loyal to Halkins, his mentor and captain.

“You will see, my boy, if you join with me. Don’t you dare think about telling old Halkins about our little talk. If you do, you lose my offer…” George set Wilam down, bending closer to his ear. “Think about it. I know you will make the right decision.”

“If not?” Wilam inquired quietly.

“You die,” the man drew his small dagger across Wilam’s neck, barely brushing the bitter blade against his skin.

Chapter Five

That night was calm on the ocean with a clear sky and a full moon. John Halkins stood on the deck with the sextant, holding it up to the stars. He lowered it slightly and glanced at the man to his right.

"We are about two more days from where our sources say the ship comes from, and returns to...the north east." Halkins said to his first mate. "According to my charts, Jenkins, there is nothing but sea out here,"

"Is that not a little vague, Captain?" Jenkins asked, "The ship may not even be out here,"

"Aye, true," Halkins brought the sextant up to his face once more. "But if my studies are correct, there is more than water out here. There is an uncharted island,"

"How do you know this, Captain?" Jenkins questioned.

"My man, I know nothing. However, I know the signs of land when I see them." He paused. "Finding this ship has been my mission for years, Jenkins, and I intend to complete it,"

"Pardon me for asking, Cap, but why?" Jenkins asked, leaning on the balustrade. "Why do you want this so bad?"

Halkins lowered the instrument again and was silent for a long while.

"Six years ago, I was friends with a man; a captain by the name of Drake. He was strange, always talking to himself. He had a dark past, I believe, for his bitter spirit divided us. We got into an argument. He left in a rage, vowing revenge on me. I came back to port, my port, to find that my home had been torched. My wife, my child…dead." Halkins drew a shaky breath; he closed his eyes.

Both men were silent.

"So…" continued Halkins, "I have been pursuing him ever since. But…he disappeared. I lost my lead. Now, however, I think the black sailed ship and the missing ships have something to do with him. I must find him. I want justice to be served."

Both men waited a moment in silence before drifting back to their quarters.

Chapter Six

The full moon shone silver over the ocean and cast moon shadows over the deck. In her dark cloak, Kathryn looked around for any of the crew. No one was in sight. She hurried over to the rigging and started to climb up. About eight meters up, she became grateful that she was barefoot and that she wore trousers that she had brought from the tavern in the harbor. Ever since she was a little girl watching the seamen in the harbor, she had always wanted to climb the rigging up to the crow's nest. Her father had always forbidden her to do so, for she was a 'proper young lady' and wasn't fit to go climbing as if she was a boy.

The mast swayed as she got higher up, and she clutched the tar-slicked ratlines with cold fingers. Her heart pounded. This was the most exhilarating thing she had ever done in her life! She actually smiled. It was fun!

Kathryn looked down to see how high she was and laughed. She wasn't even halfway up the mast, yet the deck looked miles away. She enjoyed every second of her adventure, never even considering that if she fell, she could instantly die.

At last Kathryn pulled her shaky legs up over the side of the crow's nest and tumbled inside. The wooden 'nest' was larger than Kathryn imagined it would be. It swayed slightly when she tried to stand, so she contented herself with sitting.

The sky was clear that night, with a calm breeze from the southeast to gently propel the *Farrow* through the glassy, azure waters. Kathryn inhaled the salty air deeply. Her father loved nights like this. Calm. Serene. Peaceful. Clear. He would go out on the deck every translucent night to watch for falling stars.

Kathryn hugged her knees to her chest, looking at the sky. Was her father looking at those very stars? Was he thinking of his daughter as she was thinking of him? Or was he even alive anymore?

Kathryn sighed, sadly. So many unanswered questions. So few answers.

Suddenly, she became very aware of something around her. Something bigger than her. It wasn’t at all frightening, but on the contrary; comforting, protecting, shielding.

“Hello,” she whispered to the stars, “I don’t know who or what you are. I need help. I'm scared. I can't do this alone. Please.”

She broke down in tears.

Chapter Seven

Wilam was perched on the foremast at the front of the ship, watching the small, cloaked figure climb carefully down from the mainmast. Kathryn had been up in the crow's nest for nigh an hour, and Wilam had been waiting for her.

He skimmed down the mast and landed silently on the deck with his bare feet. After tugging on his boots, he walked over to the foot of the mainmast as Kathryn came to the end of the ratlines, planning to offer to help her down. Three meters above the deck, Kathryn lost her footing on the wet, tar-covered ropes and cried out as she began to fall.

All of a sudden, Kathryn found herself in the arms of Wilam Eugene, who was almost as surprised as she.

"Thank you, Wilam," Kathryn said, feeling rather foolish.

After he set her down, Wilam smiled sheepishly and shrugged.

"I watched you go up to the crow's nest," he explained, "I wanted to ask you something,"

"Yes?" Kathryn inquired, pulling the cloak around her to hide the trousers that she was wearing.

"I…I…" he suddenly lost all courage to ask her the question he had been wanting to request of her. "Do you enjoy the *Farrow*?" he blurted instead.

"Yes," she said, "I love it,"

"The men aren't bothering you?" the young man looked intently at her face. She was gazing towards the sea on the port side; the full moon illuminating her features radiantly.

"Not all of them," she teased.

"Who is, then?" he inquired, not getting her joke.

"You," she burst out laughing and Wilam smiled again. Kathryn giggled one last time, grateful to be able to laugh away her stress for a few moments. "Good night, Wilam Eugene,"

Wilam watched her disappear below deck, remembering when his own mother used to say 'good night' to him before he went to bed.

Chapter Eight

Friday,

The captain Halkins thought we would reach our destination yesterday, but the winds are harsh and the waves rough. The calm night on day four was foreshadowing the storm that was brewing. Such is the sea; unpredictable and grey. All day it has been a dull grey. The ship tosses and turns and for the first time in my life, I believe I am a bit seasick! The crew battles the wind at the ship's sails while I am cooped below deck in my little barrel room with only books for company. I would rather be above deck. The rats are starting to worry me. ~Kathryn B. Thatcher

Kathryn placed the charcoal and her journal into a leather satchel she kept by her side. Sighing, she picked up a worn, red book with tattered pages. Opening it, she curled up on her pile of blankets in the corner, and began to read.

Wilam struggled with the sails, trying to tie one end that had come loose.

"Tie it well," Halkins had said earlier, "lest the wind take down a mast,"

Wilam's wet hair and clothes were plastered to his body, and he shivered from the cold. Jack also was soaking wet from the rainsquall. He crouched on the deck, securing the mast along with numerous crewmembers. The tempest was greater than ever.

The ship pitched and rolled over the ocean swells. Waves crashed over the decks, nearly sweeping several sailors off into the billowing sea. Below deck Kathryn could barely keep her footing. She placed her most cherished belongings in an old leather satchel. She slung it over her shoulder in the occasion that she would have to leave the hold quickly, such as if the ship began to sink.

The men struggled to keep the ship afloat as the waves grew bigger. The sky grew nearly black with the thick storm clouds. The wind raged violently, casting down torrents of rain, while lightning flashed and thunder roared in the atmosphere.

Wilam could not even see his hand in front of him, blindly fighting the wind. He grabbed the foremast, struggling to shield his face from the water that slapped brutally at him. He hugged the slick wood to keep himself from falling into the icy waves.

Suddenly, he looked behind at the mainmast, his stomach twisting. He scrambled down from his perch on the foremast, shouting for help from his fellow crewmates.

John Halkins heard the sickening *crack* like the sound of wood splintering. The ship tilted as the heavy main mast began to lean to port side. Halkins yelled suddenly as he slipped and slid over the wet deck to help the men try to save the mast. He pulled at the ropes, amid the crewmembers, his back muscles straining. If the mast fell, the ship would turn over, spelling the end of the *Farrow.*

Chapter Nine

Monday,

The Farrow *is in terrible shape. Her main mast is broken and leans the entire ship over from port side. With no wind and no oars, we cannot continue our journey or even go for help. The mast cannot be repaired at sea! The storm threw us off course and Captain John Halkins and his first mate, James Jenkins, have had trouble finding out where we are exactly. The food is being rationed very sparingly. If we do not get help soon…I fear the worst.*
~Kathryn B. Thatcher

Behind her wall of barrels down in the hold, Kathryn wrote glumly in her journal. With the ship tilted at an odd angle, not all stayed orderly on any of the decks.

Silently, Wilam crept through the carpenter's hall. His hazel brown eyes adjusted to the dimness as he felt his way down the lower decks, down to the hold. With the mast broken, there wasn't much he could do on the disabled *Farrow*, for he was a sails man: one who patched and handled the sails. He came to the door that led to the hold, gently opening it and stepping inside. He closed it behind him and then stopped as a sound reached his ears. Creeping closer to the source of the noise, he sat down hushed, leaning his back against the barrels.

"*How standest thou, so mighty and great; dost thou not realize thy humblest fate? To be slain by a peasant, wretched and poor; to destroy thy pride whist naught but a sword; How standest thou; Now so low and defeated? Beware! Lest thy dying be repeated!*" Kathryn paused, listening closely around her, aware of a presence in the hold near her. "You can come out," she said after a moment, "I can hear you breathing,"

Sheepishly, Wilam crawled out to the 'entrance' of her makeshift room.

"Hello, Wilam," she said.

"Miss Thatcher," he returned the greeting. "You were reading," he commented in subtle admiration.

"Aye, yes," she laughed, holding the book out to him. "My father loved poetry."

"And taught you to read, also?" Wilam assumed. He took the red book reverently. He had never touched a book in his life. He had seen them…years ago, but never touched one.

"Yes," she said. "Wilam?"

"Aye?"

"Can you read?" she asked quietly. He fingered the fragile papers, flipping through them. The little black marks jumbled together in horizontal lines on the page, his illiterate eyes making no sense of them. Quietly he closed it and held it out to Kathryn.

"Nay," he hesitated.

"What is it, Wilam?" she asked again. Wilam suddenly lost his courage yet again to ask her his question.

"You know the captain's mission," he said, and then looked into Kathryn's green eyes.

"Yes. To find the black-sailed ship and all of the missing vessels, too."

"The crew knows it."

"Yes, so?"

"Most are afraid. They think we will go missing, too."

"Nonsense," Kathryn shrugged. "Captain Halkins is a wonderful, skilled captain."

"Aye, he is. The best I've worked for in my life," Wilam tilted his head and looked at the girl sitting across from him. "What do you think about the black-sailed sloop?"

"They took my papa, Wilam,"

"You say you saw the captain?"

"Aye, yes. He was dreadful," she said, her eyebrows wrinkling together in confusion. Why was he asking these questions? "Why do you ask about him?"

"Miss Thatcher," he began, looking down, "The captain of the black sailed ship is my uncle,"

Chapter Ten

"Captain," wheezing, Jack stumbled over to the captain who stood at the forecastle with a spyglass in his hand. "There's a ship on the horizon,"

"Aye."

"She has black sails, sir."

"Aye," The captain was amazingly calm. He said not another word but raised the spyglass to his eye.

"What do we do, sir?"

"We cannot do anything, my man," Halkins lowered the glass and looked at Jack with sad, blue eyes. "but raise the white flag."

"To surrender, sir?" Jack asked, incredulous.

"Aye. Unless you can fire a cannon and fight these pirates with a weakened and starved crew as mine."

Halkins motioned to two men arguing a few meters away.

"Stop drinking the provisions, Maynard," the thin one was saying to the chubby, cherub-faced man. "Were running out of drink as it is wi'out ye getting drunk on it,"

"What you mean? There be drink all around us!" Maynard slurred, taking a swig of his mug.

"That be salt water, mate."

"Don't make no difference," Maynard staggered about the deck and then fell over the side, splashing into the water. His companion sighed and then went to retrieve Maynard with the lifeboat.

"Aye, sir. I'll go put up the flag." Jack turned and left the captain to raise the white flag. In the background, George stood nearby, sharpening his cutlass and listening to Halkins and Jack. He smiled malevolently, his narrow yellowed teeth gleaming in the sunlight. The large, bald man glanced out at the black-sailed galleon and held up the cutlass blade to the sun, admiring its gleam. *This is a good, good day*, he thought to himself.

Chapter Eleven

"What?" Kathryn stood abruptly, her notebook falling to the floor. Wilam stood also, suddenly regretting telling his secret. He took a step towards her.

"Miss Thatcher…"

"Don't come any closer, Wilam," she commanded, her voice quavering. "Whose side are you on?"

"Listen, Miss Thatcher," he begged, "You must try to understand. I am not on that pirate's side," he hesitated.

"Continue."

"Listen, I never had a father. I was born on a ship. I then lived with my mother in a tiny village, far from New Harbour. When I was eight, she died from the cholera and I was placed in the care of her older brother. He was a captain of a ship and I was his cabin boy under his care. He was horribly cruel, and I was whipped several times for my inept ability to fulfill all of his commands. He was a pirate on the sea and always had big plans…"

"What kind of plans?" Kathryn interrupted.

"Something with black sails. I never heard all of the plans. They were always spoken of behind closed doors. I was thirteen when we were in port in the city of New Harbour, when I decided to escape that ship. I disappeared, and I haven't seen him since," he hesitated, "I am not good for anything other than working on a ship, so I came to the *Farrow*. I was born on the sea, you know. They say 'What is of the sea, will always return to the sea.'"

"Does that have anything to do with the tattoo on your back?" she snapped. He looked at her sharply, his eyes flashing.

"Possibly," he said through clenched teeth.

"How do you know, then, that he is the captain of the black-sailed ship?"

"You drew this, did you not?" From his shirt, he withdrew her parchment and charcoal portrayal of the sloop and the captain's face next to it.

"Indeed," she gasped, astonished, "But Wilam, I gave that to Captain Halkins!"

"Aye," Wilam narrowed his eyes.

"Did he give it to you?"

"That is none of your concern," Wilam snapped. "All I know is that this is the face of my uncle and his ship. Three rows of oars, right?"

"You stole that from the captain's desk, didn't you?" Kathryn clenched her fists against her side, her knuckles turning white. "Whose side are you *really* on, Wilam?"

"Does it matter anymore, Kathryn Thatcher? If you haven't noticed, the *Farrow* isn't in top shape." Frustrated, Wilam turned away from her.

"So you really are joining the mutiny, are you not?"

"How do you know about the mutiny?" Wilam asked, looking at her sharply. She narrowed her eyes and stepped back, her hand reaching down to her knife she kept at her side.

"Does it matter anymore, *Wilam Eugene*?" she retorted. Wilam opened his mouth to say something back to her when the ship jerked roughly, toppling Kathryn and Wilam to the ground. Kathryn cried out, grabbing her journal and her book of poetry. The two young people stumbled over one another, trying to grab a hold of anything to pull them back onto their feet. Wilam grasped Kathryn's hand and helped her to her feet.

"What's going on?" Kathryn cried, then jerked her hand away. Wilam knew no more than she did, and he frantically searched for the door that led out of the hold. His mind felt muddled and dizzy from the sudden jerking of the ship, its odd movements catching him off guard whenever he found a foothold.

"Come on," Wilam took hold of her arm and the two half-walked, half-stumbled to the exit, unaware of the danger they were walking into.

Chapter Twelve

The black sailed galleon quickly pulled up parallel to the *Farrow.* Men swarmed onto the crooked deck, all with some sort of black on them. Black scarf. Black shirt. Black handkerchief around the head. They all brandished weapons. Halkins stood in front of his crew, his back straight, his hands clasped behind his back, and his chin slightly tilted up.

A man appeared from the masses of the black-clad pirates. He carried himself proudly, dressed in the dark color of his crew. However, something was odd, Halkins thought. This man's face was not anything like the depiction Kathryn had drawn on her parchment. This fact did not prevent the fear that the man's aura provoked, nor did it make him any less frightening. His tall figure was clad in a black coat, like what Kathryn had described, and from a leather strap dangled four pistols. His face was gaunt and pale, with hollow black eyes that stared hideously at the humble crew of the *Farrow.*

"You surrender?" he was the first to break the silence that had settled over the deck as he directed the question towards Halkins.

"Aye," Halkins said in a tense voice. "We cannot fight. We cannot sail. We are incapable of repairing our mast. We surrender."

"Such the disappointment..." the wan man said, rather sadly. "I was looking forward to a good fight with plenty of slaughter and bloodshed. But, no matter,"

His voice suddenly grew cruel.

"Bind these men," he commanded. The pirates swarmed around the crew of the *Farrow.* The man pointed a long, gnarly finger at Halkins. "We will save him for the Admiral."

Halkins was forced to his knees and bound rashly with cord by a large, burly pirate with a thick, pocked nose and wormy lips. The rest of the crew on deck, fifty-three men in all, were also subdued and bound back-to-back with one another as the sallow leader of the pirates ordered the black ship to turn it's stern to the *Farrow.*

Jack struggled against his restraints, trying to reach his knife he kept in his trousers. A slender pirate, no older than Wilam, struck Jack in the jaw and then ripped the dagger from Jack's bound hands. Jack clenched his teeth together as the young pirate laughed wickedly at his expense. The pirate had well-kempt blonde hair that hung in his blue eyes and straight, white teeth. He was well fed, as were each of the other pirates on the black ship. Jack thought this odd, for most seamen were not very well nourished at sea, and certainly not pirates. This boy was not a seaman.

Meanwhile, the black ship had backed her stern to the fore of the *Farrow.* More men from on the galleon threw over several hooked anchors attached to ropes that were connected to the black galleon's body. The pirates fastened the anchors around the *Farrow,* securing them around the ship carefully.

"Alright!" the leader called to the black-sailed ship. Jack looked up from his sitting position as the ship's three rows of oars swiftly commenced in unison to propel her forward. The *Farrow* groaned slightly, then jerked forward at her odd angle. The leader of the black-sailed galleon frowned. "She'll need repairs done," he muttered to George, who had been surveying the ship's activities meditatively. "But I think she'll do,"

Jack overheard him, and the ship jerked clumsily again. He wondered what the man meant by his remark, and he also wondered what George had to do with anything. He had known that George was not a loyal man to the *Farrow*. No ship had a completely trustworthy crew, but what did he have to do with anything about the black ship and its leader?

"Why don't you just kill us now?" Jack snarled sarcastically to the leader. He tried to shift to a more comfortable position as the pallid face peered down on him.

The tip of a cutlass blade slowly stroked Jack's throat. He drew in a breath, watching the blade with wide blue eyes. "Young man, if it were my choice, I would have killed you all and sunk your sorry ship for the sheer joy of watching you die. Unfortunately, my orders were to return with a full ship and crew. However…I don't think one brash young man will matter much if he is inexplicably missing. Don't tempt me."

The cutlass withdrew, and Jack remained silent. However, he wondered about their fate. Why were they prisoners? Another thought came to his mind.

*His orders were...*Jack thought, *He's taking orders from someone. But who?* The *Farrow* jerked again as the pirate ship dragged it through the water, gradually gaining speed.

Chapter Thirteen

"Something's wrong," Wilam said, halting to a stop in the carpenter's hall of the ship.

"Of course something's wrong;" Kathryn muttered.

"We're moving," Wilam noted with bewilderment. "How?"

"I was about to ask you the same." Kathryn yanked her arm free from Wilam's vice grip and brushed off the cover of her book. She affectionately placed it next to her journal in her leather satchel. "It is also deathly silent…on all decks,"

"Aye," Wilam said. "I don't believe that it is safe out there."

"What could possibly be going on?" Kathryn asked, timidly. She was starting to realize the eerie situation. The ship jerked again, and Wilam lost his balance, lurching towards Kathryn. He stopped himself by planting his hands on the wall on either side of her. Her face was inches from his.

Crossly, she pushed him away, and he balanced himself on the other wall across from her.

"Sorry," he murmured. Kathryn huffed.

"Please, get us out of here," she said. Nodding, Wilam proceeded onward down the darkened hall. The carpenter's hall was an antechamber built into the ship between the hull and the lower decks. Its purpose was to grant the ship's carpenters a way to scrutinize the hull of the ship easily and efficiently and to check for compulsory repairs. Ordinarily, it was unoccupied, but sometimes it provided the perfect place for a clandestine murder.

Wilam and Kathryn got out of the hallway and onto the third deck. The cannons on port side were facing down to the water from the angle at which the ship lay. The two young people scanned the room, and, not locating any sort of life, they progressed onto the next deck above, steadily growing closer to danger than they realized. As they approached the main deck, Wilam stopped.

"Wait," Wilam said, holding up his hand. Kathryn tucked a stray curl of hair behind her ear and nodded silently.

"Do you hear voices?" he whispered.

"Shhh…" Kathryn put a finger to her lips and silenced him.

Indeed, coming from above them were harsh voices, arguing amongst one another. Their speech was muffled, and neither Kathryn, nor Wilam could make out what they were saying through the wooden floor above them.

"I'm going on deck to see what this is all about," Wilam whispered, rising to his feet. The ship had stopped its spontaneous jolting for the most part, and for this, Kathryn was grateful.

"But," she started to protest, then stopped. She nodded, hesitantly. "All right. I will come with you."

"No, stay down here," Wilam ordered, looking at her sharply. What kind of a girl was she? It was dangerous above deck. Something was not right.

"I refuse to be left down here alone." Kathryn said determinedly.

"Kathryn…" he scowled.

"I'm going." she pushed past him, and then felt his rough hand on her shoulder.

"If you are, then stay behind me," he said. She silently complied and followed him. He did not look back at her, so she did not see his quiet smile of admiration.

Chapter Fourteen

The black-sailed ship was moving steadily now, smoothly towing the disabled *Farrow* through the glassy sea. A gentle breeze came from the southeast, filling the wicked black sails with wind and helping to propel her on her journey. The sun was high in the sky at mid-afternoon, and the scorching heat palpitated on the prisoners of the *Farrow*. They sat in constrained groups around the deck, hardly able to move through their restraints that bound their ankles and wrists. Sweat poured from the confined prisoners, as tongues grew swollen and parched from thirst.

Halkins's blue eyes were shut tight under his restricting blindfold. His limbs were numb and lifeless. Even if he were unbound, he didn't think he would be able to move.

Water. All he wanted was a little water.

“We near our destination,” the pale commander of the black ship said from his shady corner of the poop deck. Earlier, he had introduced himself as Edmund Maldone before the prisoners were all blindfolded. George sat by his side, a black band around his thick arm.

Keeping an eye on the prisoners, George sharpened his cutlass, remaining silent as Maldone droned on and on about something. He was growing quite peeved with this sickly-skinned man. George knew he would be a much better leader of the black ship. Thinking this, he stopped whetting his blade. He scanned the perspiring faces of the prisoners, looking for one in particular. Not locating him, George stood, his fist closing around his weapon as he put it in his sheath.

“What is it, comrade?” Maldone asked, nonchalantly spitting chewing tobacco out of the side of his mouth.

George didn’t answer. Without a word, he walked around the deck, and then came to the entrance that led below decks. He reached his calloused hand out to open the door, when suddenly it whipped open on its own.

Wilam saw the face of his rival before George saw him. Wilam inadvertently gave a small cry of anguish when George reached down and grabbed the front of his shirt, hauling the young man up onto the main deck. George then noticed the girl. Swiftly, he lunged for her, dragging Wilam in his strapping clutches. Kathryn gave a shriek as the massive bald man managed to grab the base of her long dark braid. Her leather bag that contained her notebook fell to the deck from her shoulder and slid unnoticed into a corner.

Jerking the two teenagers out of the dimness of the lower deck, George slammed the door shut behind them. Paralyzed from terror, Wilam and Kathryn remained submissive and silent. Their captor altered his hold on them so he was gripping them by their shoulders. Maldone stood from his seat as the posse came towards him.

"What…"

"Sir, these are two more prisoners who got missed in the search."

Maldone took a second glance at Kathryn.

"A girl?" he asked, incredulous. "They have a woman on their wretched ship?"

Several pirates from the black sailed ship who were guarding the captives looked towards their leader at his outburst. They too, stared in astonishment at the girl.

One of them, the young blonde thug who had struck Jack, looked attentively at Kathryn. He cocked his head, causing his long blonde hair to fall over his forehead, and stared at her. She shifted uneasily under his intense gaze and bit her lip nervously.

"Such a pretty thing," Maldone commented, raising a thin eyebrow. Wilam let out a low rumble in his throat, a small growl like that of a dog. "Bind them with the others," Maldone commanded George. "We will disembark at our destination in a short while."

Kathryn glanced at the black-sailed ship that was towing the *Farrow*. Beyond the bow of the ship, she saw a rather large strip of land…an island. George finished tying Wilam's wrists together and forced him to kneel on the deck with the other prisoners, and then turned to Kathryn. She winced as the rough ropes were yanked tight across her wrists. The man forced her, also, to kneel on the deck across from Wilam. His hazel brown eyes met her emerald green ones in a silent anxious gaze before they were blindfolded along with the others.

Chapter Fifteen

The crescent-shaped island was covered in tropical nature for most of its large span with vast quantities of flora and fauna, including an enormous array of foliage. Palm, coconut, plantain, banana, mango, and so many other fruits produced by the trees provided food and cover for the wildlife that ran under the cover of the hierarchy of vegetation. Wild hogs and goats roamed freely around the island, providing the inhabitants with an occasional feast of meat.

The city was immense with buildings being erected all around. A harbor, a small village, a market, could all be seen in the region of the falcate bay of the island. People milled about the city. Several groups of men were shackled together in slave chains either standing in long lines, or building the surrounding architecture. Red flags were positioned everywhere in the metropolis; all displaying the insignia of the silhouette of the black-sailed ship.

The black galleon began to pull into the crescent bay of the island and approached the pier dock. It was immediately surrounded by men of all ages to help pull it by its ropes into the harbor. Other men hauled in the mutilated *Farrow*, detaching her from the black galleon.

The pirates went around the deck, removing the blindfolds from the captives' eyes.

Kathryn stared, taking in the sights of the city. The red flags caught her eye. The black emblem of a ship struck her as familiar. Suddenly, an image of the tattoo on Wilam's left shoulder came to Kathryn's memory. They were one and the same.

As the black-sailed ship landed and anchored in the harbor bay, the prisoners were herded together once their feet were freed from their constraints. George, however, jerked Kathryn by her bound arms away from the masses of the Farrow crew.

"You ain't going with them, girl," he snarled. She cast a fleeting look of despair into Wilam's hazel brown eyes before they were wrenched around, unable to see one another anymore. There was a crowd of men on the harbor dock in the bay who grabbed the ropes of the wrecked *Farrow*, pulling it to the dock. Once moored, the gangplank was lowered to the ground and the captives herded forward. Kathryn was the last one to disembark, escorted by Maldone and George. Kathryn noticed that the blonde pirate kept looking back at her as he pushed the prisoners down the cobbled streets along with the other pirates.

"Where are they taking them?" she cried, as George and Maldone began leading her down a different road than the others went. "Where are you taking me?"

"Shut up, girl," George snarled. Kathryn began to panic.

"What's going on? Where are you taking me? What is this place?" she looked around desperately trying to get a glance of Halkins or Wilam. She jerked around, but George maintained his grasp on her arm.

"I said, shut up!" he yelled, pulling his hand back and striking her across the cheek. Tears sprang into her eyes as her face grew red from the sting. Maldone walked on the other side of her, glancing at her, as she grew pensively silent. Kathryn bit her lip and willed herself not to cry. Common people passed by the men and Kathryn.

Some gave her a second glance. They were all dressed in rather old-fashioned clothes, and they all had a sort of troubled look in their eyes. It was like they were living in constant fear for their lives. Perhaps they were.

They turned off the main road down a path that took them uphill. In time, they came to a grand building. It was very large and sat upon the hill overlooking the entire island bay. Built out of slate-grey stone with golden wood for a roof, the building faced the north. Windows from top to bottom faced the east side of it. Kathryn subtly glanced back towards the sea. Through the palm trees, the house overlooked the bay where the black ship and *Farrow* had arrived. Walking along the grassy yard, Maldone, George, and Kathryn came to the entrance. A man stood on the terrace facing away from them, looking out on the bay. His arms were crossed over his chest. He wore a billowy white shirt, black trousers, and a blood-red scarf for a belt. He turned towards the group, and Kathryn gasped when she saw his face. It was the man who had taken her father. The man who had destroyed her ship. The man on the black-sailed ship who had placed her on the sinking frigate and sailed away.

Her bound hands clenched into fists behind her back.

His face was the same as she had drawn it. Long, black hair, graying at the temples, was neatly parted and plaited to his broad shoulders. His beard was still the same style from years before, but now it had turned grey with only a streak of youthful black left at the chin. His face was more weathered too, showing signs of age. His eyes remained unchanging…stormy silver. They flickered with a slight hint of recognition when they glanced at Kathryn, but he turned to Maldone and George.

"George!" the man's face broke into what could be called a smile. Kathryn saw it as cold and heartless. George nodded and shook the man's extended hand.

"Pleasure, Admiral,"

"Good to see you again. Did you succeed with the *Farrow*?"

"Aye, sir. We only just arrived."

"Aye, so I see. How bad is the ship's condition?"

"Slight. Merely a snapped mainmast, sir."

"Acceptable. We will place the vessel in for repairs immediately." The Admiral turned to Maldone. "And you? How was your fare?"

"Good. No trouble at all, save an unexpected occurrence in the plan," Maldone jerked his pale head towards Kathryn who was standing between George and Maldone. The Admiral shifted his tempestuous silver gaze to the girl.

"I see. The issue?"

"We did not anticipate a girl to be amid the crew."

"Aye. T'would be an unforeseen concern." The Admiral stared at her for a moment before cupping her chin in his icy hand and tilting her face towards the light. She cringed. He turned her head, examining her facial features. Kathryn fought the urge to pull away from his cold fingers. He let go of her chin and stroked his beard. "I never forget a face," he said, thoughtfully. "Aye, I remember now. I set you on that useless navy frigate about five years ago, am I correct?"

"Aye, sir," Kathryn whispered, terrified. How could he remember that?

"You were…how old? Eleven, was it?"

"Aye," she said again; her voice was barely audible.

"How many years are you now?"

"Sixteen, sir."

"Your name?"

"Kathryn...Kathryn Thatcher,"

"Lovely young woman you are, Miss Thatcher. Beautiful. Pray, tell me, how do you come to be on a humble frigate as the *Farrow*?"

"Looking for my father, sir," she stammered nervously. She didn't trust this man.

"Your father?" he inquired, leaning against the wall of the granite building.

"Thomas Thatcher. You took him prisoner that day you set me on the sinking ship," Kathryn said, gaining courage to speak bolder.

"The name sounds familiar," the Admiral waved off George and Maldone. "Thank you, men. That will be all for today. George, I need you to locate and situate the new prisoners. Maldone, you may return to your crew. You are dismissed."

The men left, leaving Kathryn alone on the terrace with the Admiral.

"You want to find your father," he commented, chuckling.

"Is he alive?" Kathryn asked fervently.

"Aye, well, he's not dead."

"What do you want with him?" Kathryn cried. "And with the crew of the *Farrow*?"

The Admiral turned and grabbed his black coat that was lying on a bush. He shrugged it on and started walking up the path...a different way than the other men had gone. "Follow me, Miss Thatcher,"

Wrists still bound together, Kathryn followed the man wearily. She felt utterly exhausted from all that had happened that day. All she wanted to do was go to sleep. Her steps faltered as she climbed higher up the peak behind the Admiral. He halted at the highest climax of the hill and looked down at Kathryn. As she staggered up the last few strides, the Admiral wrapped his cold fingers around her shoulders and faced her in the direction of the bay. She saw the city with its silhouetted flags as the sun dipped lower in the sky, illuminating the endless sea.

"What do you see, Miss Thatcher?"

"T-the city, sir,"

"Aye. I built this conurbation," he said slowly, "My beautiful island capital."

Hands still grasping her shoulders, the Admiral faced the girl the other way...towards the south. She gasped, terrified at what she saw.

"Take a good, long look, my dear," he whispered. His breath was hot on her ear. "Behold, my army."

Chapter Sixteen

Kathryn stared. Surrounding the southernmost parts of the island were ships. So many different kinds of ships: frigates and galleons, sloops and clippers…and all were black. There were nearly forty of them. Two were moored on the sandy beaches on their sides, having their barnacles removed. The workers were being led away from the work site as it was nearing twilight.

Looking closer at the scene, Kathryn noticed that the workers were not merely hired hands, but slaves. A large man was directing them with a whip.

"What is this?" Kathryn asked, aghast and faintly nauseated by what she saw.

"My vast brigand fleet of black ships." he laughed evilly. "Once it is complete, I will strike terror into the hearts of nations, ruling them however I please,"

"So this is where all of the ships go that disappear from New Harbour," Kathryn whispered.

"Aye, the men also. I usually try to…refrain from killing men, as that gives me more hands to construct my city, paint and repair my ships, and, if qualified, become one with my militia."

"Then why…" Kathryn frowned, looking to the man. His skin glowed golden from the luminescence of the mounted torch behind him, "Then why did you destroy the ship that I was on? Why did you kill dozens of able sailors?"

"Ah," the Admiral shifted his eyes to meet hers. "That was an exceptional state of affairs. Three navy ships found my island and destroyed five of my black vessels. I only had ten at the time. I vowed revenge on those three ships. Your vessel was one of them, Miss Thatcher."

Kathryn suddenly remembered her father's terror of the black sailed ship when it pursued the *Princess Anne* those many years ago. She hadn't completely understood her father's fear then, but she did now. Her father knew that the ship would be coming after them. She did not remember when the navy had destroyed the black ships, as the Admiral told her now, because she had not been on the *Princess Anne* at the time of the fight.

Twilight was enveloping the sky in a violet haze as the moon gleamed brightly over the island; the moonbeams surrounded the island's metropolis in the dusky shade of the night. Stars were beginning to reveal themselves through the azure curtain of the heavens. Torches began to flare up in the streets of the city, casting flickering shadows on the buildings. The streets befell deathly silent with only the gentle rustling of the tropics and the rush of the sea to be heard.

Kathryn's legs nearly collapsed under her from exhaustion.

"You are silent. What are you thinking, little prisoner?" the Admiral asked, his voice low. The girl didn't answer, but instead, sank to her knees, grateful to rest her somnolent body for a moment. The Admiral noticed. "Answer me." he commanded. Kathryn looked at him in fear. His voice had dropped and he was glaring at her.

"I…I am exhausted," she whispered.

"Perhaps you should retire with the others," he commented, amused.

"Perhaps…" she distantly thought of Wilam. He would be with the others, wouldn't he?

"Ah," the Admiral said as a shadowed outline of a figure approached them. "Here he comes now,"

Into the torchlight stepped the young, blonde pirate from the black-sailed ship, the one who had struck Jack and stared at Kathryn on the ship with such interest. He was about sixteen or seventeen, and fine looking with a strong, square jaw and blue eyes. His fair hair was straight but combed back from his forehead. A dark red shirt was worn over his broad chest, along with brown trousers and black, knee-high boots.

"Sir, the prisoners are secure, fed, and watered," the young man said to the Admiral. Kathryn narrowed her eyes. The adolescent pirate made the prisoners sound like they were livestock.

"Excellent. Rafe, this is yet another of the prisoners, aye?"

"Aye, sir," the teenager called Rafe looked Kathryn over, a grin forming on his lips.

"Take this young lady to the accommodations at once. She is fatigued," the Admiral pointed to the girl.

She stood, all her muscles screaming against the movement.

"Aye, sir."

"Let her rest. She has a full day tomorrow," the Admiral nodded. Kathryn cringed as the boy named Rafe took her arm to support her and led her away down the dim, torch-lit road. She looked back once. The Admiral watched them until they turned out of sight, his silver eyes narrowing.

Chapter Seventeen

Kathryn's abhorrence to the young man called Rafe increased with every step they took. He walked exceedingly close to her at her side, holding a torch in his opposite hand from her. She cursed the fact that her hands were still bound together and her knife was under her tattered dress, strapped to her calf.

Rafe watched her out of the corner of his eye. *Indeed*, he thought to himself, *she is a beautiful creature*.

"Rafe Norrington," he said to her. "What is your name?"

She didn't acknowledge him but stared straight ahead. Rafe didn't take lightly to being ignored. He suddenly grabbed her shoulder and twisted her around to face him.

"Unhand me!" Kathryn screamed angrily with a fury and vigor she didn't know she still had. "Your orders were to take me to my accommodations and nothing more. Unhand me!"

Irritated and irked, Rafe let go of her shoulder. He pushed her, indicating she should move forward. Too furious to be afraid, Kathryn glared into his eyes and walked on.

Presently, they arrived at a large, low building, like a stable. It was on the outskirts of town down a dirt trail and illuminated by no more than five dying torches. Few trees surrounded the clearing.

Taking a key from his pocket, Rafe clicked it into the chained lock of the thick, wooden doors. As they stepped inside, Kathryn saw iron-barred cells on the right and left of the oblong room, leaving a small, dirt path to walk between them. The atmosphere was dank and humid, saturated by musty, stale air. Kathryn gulped the fresh air of the outside before Rafe shut the door behind them. By the light of his torch, Rafe led Kathryn down the rows of cells. Kathryn saw several crewmembers of the *Farrow* as they passed by, but they all appeared to be sleeping and didn't look up.

Kathryn felt a sickening pang in her gut when she didn't see Wilam.

Rafe led Kathryn to a cell at the very end of the structure next to an empty cell. He opened it, and Kathryn stepped inside, drained of all her strength.

"Give me your hands," he commanded, withdrawing his dagger.

"No," she said, not knowing what he was going to do. Without another word, he whipped her around and grabbed her hands that were bound behind her back. He slipped the sharp blade around the ropes and they clipped off of her bruised wrists. Throwing a hard loaf of bread to her, Rafe slammed the cell door shut, locked it tight, and then left the building. The prison was enclosed in darkness.

Chapter Eighteen

A small ray of dim sunlight filtered in through the cracks of the prison, shedding some light in the gloom. Kathryn blinked her eyes and didn't move from her hard bed. Her eyelids drifted closed once more, and she sighed.

"Miss Thatcher?" a voice asked from the cell across from Kathryn. Instantly, she was awake and grabbed onto the bars of her cell, trying to make out the figure.

"Wilam?" she asked hopefully.

"Nay…Jack. They took Wilam and the captain. I don't know why. They haven't been here all night."

"Oh," dejectedly, Kathryn sighed, "Are you all right? Did they hurt you in any way?"

A laugh.

"They had a time with the whip a bit. Just to make sure we all had a pleasurable time and obeyed all the rules. Apparently, hitting a guard is against the regulations," Jack chuckled again. "What about you? What happened to you?"

Kathryn told him all that had happened and what she had found out about the Admiral.

"Jack, he's building a huge, pirate fleet with the stolen ships!" she finished.

He was silent for a while. The murky light found a space in the stone walls of the drafty prison and brightened it considerably. Kathryn could now see Jack. He was lying on his stomach, his head facing her, on the hard, wooden cot provided in all the cells. His shirt was off, and Kathryn could see red welts striped along his back. The swelling had gone down, but it still horrified her. She turned away, tears brimming in her green eyes.

"There isn't much we can do, Miss Thatcher," he finally said. "You said he uses the prisoners as slaves and crewmen for his own exploitation,"

"Yes,"

"I don't know," he sighed miserably.

"He said that I have 'a full day tomorrow,'" she said. Then added, "I'm scared Jack."

"Aye, so am I, Miss Thatcher,"

"Jack?"

"Aye?"

"You may call me Kathryn if you want."

Jack attempted a smile at her, when suddenly both were nearly blinded by the sunlight that flooded in when the doors of the prison were opened. Kathryn and the other prisoners squinted against the bright light.

"All captives," George's voice boomed from the doorway, Rafe Norrington at his side. "Up! Ready your sorry selves for a day of training labor. Exception is the girl, who will follow Rafe Norrington,"

Jack groaned and sat up slowly, reaching for his grey shirt. Pulling it over his head, he glanced towards Kathryn. Her face was pale and terrified when she desperately met Jack's eyes. He watched helplessly as Rafe unlocked her door and led her out of the prison. Several black-clad guards came to the cells and unlocked the other prison cells and rounded them up. Jack tried to get one last glimpse of Kathryn until a whip snapped on his raw back, causing him to yelp in pain. His back burned from the fresh wound.

"Pay attention, fool!" the guard with the whip sneered. The other guards laughed as Jack glared at them, flexing his shoulders to ward off the sting that the whip had left. The prisoners were herded out the doors to their vigorous tasks that awaited them.

Chapter Nineteen

Wilam and Halkins had been separated from the crew of the *Farrow* when they had docked. Two pirates had led them down a different path. Wilam had never seen such a well-organized metropolis such as the city they walked through now, and the complex system amazed him. The rough men who led the trio pushed them forward, forcing them to walk faster.

"Why does he want you?" Halkins asked Wilam in a low voice as they were led down the street. Wilam tried to ignore the stares he was receiving from residential onlookers. They were curious to know who the new prisoners were.

"Who?" Wilam asked, distracted by the sights.

"The captain of the black ship…what do they call him…the Admiral? Why does he want you?"

Wilam looked away, unable to make eye contact with his captain. “I…I…I don’t want you to think I have anything to do with the mutiny,” he finally stammered.

“What mutiny? On the *Farrow*?”

“Aye, sir. George was trying to convince me to join. But, sir?”

“Aye, boy?”

“The Admiral is my uncle. I'm sorry, sir. I should have told you earlier,” Wilam blurted. Suddenly, Wilam was yanked back by one of the guards.

“He be you uncle, aye?” the guard spit, holding Wilam by his tattered shirt.

“Aye,” Wilam gagged from the stench of the man’s breath. The husky man peered into Wilam’s hazel brown eyes, scowling.

“Ye ain’t got his looks, fer sure,” the man snarled. “We’ll see what he’s to say about ye tomorrow. Move it!”

Chapter Twenty

Wilam and Halkins spent the night in a small stone building, their hands chained to the wall with iron fetters. As the sun came about halfway up the morning sky, Wilam woke up groggily to the sounds of working men. The house prison they were located in was on a rocky cliff by the sea; the men he heard were the crew of prisoners scraping barnacles off of the hulls of ships.

Wilam rolled his neck around, shaking off the stiffness and discomfort of the night. Halkins was chained to Wilam's right, still snoring.

"Sir," Wilam said quietly, attempting to arouse the man. He was unsuccessful. Wilam grew quiet, absorbed by his own thoughts. He wondered what his uncle would do to him. He wondered about Kathryn.

Miserably, his head fell back against the stone building, causing stray curls of his light brown hair to tumble over his forehead. He let out a long, depressed sigh. Kathryn. He closed his eyes and imagined her face.

He had never before met a girl like her. The way she gave the impression that she disliked him made her all the more attractive to him. He smiled.

His happiness was short-lived when the door rattled open to reveal a guard in the doorway.

“Get up, men,” the giant, well-built guard announced, coming to unlock their chains. “The Admiral will see you now,”

Chapter Twenty-One

Rafe dragged Kathryn down the path she had gone up last night, towards the Admiral's house. He seemed to be in a great hurry.

"What kind of man is the Admiral?" she asked Rafe resentfully, trying to pull her arm out of his grasp. "I can walk,"

"He's like a storm on the ocean…" Rafe said. He let go of her arm and pushed her forward.

"In what way?" she asked.

"Unpredictable. One day may start beautiful and clear, and the next moment there's a hurricane." He gestured to the right. "That way,"

"Oh…" Kathryn fell silent. As they reached the top of the hill, that on which sat the stone house, Kathryn spotted the Admiral as he had been standing last night: on his terrace. Another man was standing at his side.

Kathryn looked closer at the stranger, and then gasped.

"Papa!" she cried, starting to run to him.

"Kathryn?" he turned just in time to have her collapse into his arms, weeping with joy.

"Oh, Papa, you're not dead! You aren't dead!" she sobbed into his shoulder. He embraced her tightly in his arms, a few tears falling from his own eyes as well. Finally pulling her away, he gazed at her.

"How you've grown, my Tip," he whispered. "So beautiful, like your mother…" his shoulders fell slightly as he stroked her hair and stared at her face in wonder.

Kathryn also observed her father, but with not so much admiration. His once-dark hair was now completely grey and thinning at the top. Wrinkles lined his thin, weather-beaten face. Even his green eyes looked dull. He was very thin compared to most of the men Kathryn had seen on the island, and noticeably paler.

"Papa," she murmured, grasping his hand, "What happened to you?"

"He is now part of my militia. He works on one of my ships," The Admiral, who had been standing nearby with Rafe adjacent him, had witnessed the reunion disgustedly. The man was nothing to him. The Admiral didn't even know why he had bothered to let the girl see her old man. There was obviously not much to perceive of him, and it wouldn't even do her any good to see him in his miserable state.

"What does he *do* on *your* ship? Look at him! He's half starved!" Kathryn boldly said to the Admiral.

"Tip…" her father cautioned. His voice was weak.

"He is one of my hundreds of oarsmen," the Admiral stated, crossing his arms over his splendid black coat.

"What!?" Kathryn cried. The Admiral waved his hand, and two guards appeared seemingly out of nowhere.

"That's enough family time. Men, take old Thatcher to his quarters immediately,"

Forcefully, the men separated Kathryn and her father, ignoring her protests. They roughly hauled the old man away as Kathryn was held back by Rafe to prevent her from following her father. Breathing heavily, she watched him as he was led away. A grim determination settled over her.

If I ever get off of this island, I'm taking Papa with me…away from this brutality.

"Get your hands off of me!" she snarled at Rafe. The teenager looked to the Admiral, and he nodded. Rafe let go of the girl, receiving a glare from her.

"You will take the girl back to her quarters, Rafe, and give her food and drink," the Admiral said, placing his hands behind his back and looking towards the two young people.

"Aye sir," Rafe tugged on Kathryn's elbow. Suddenly, she reached down and pulled out her knife she kept at her calf, holding it to Rafe's throat. He backed away a few steps, scowling at her.

"Don't lay another hand on me," she said.

"Idiot!" the Admiral whipped out his cutlass and started to advance towards Rafe. "I commanded you to search all prisoners and remove all weapons!"

He raised the cutlass up above his head, and Rafe sank to his knees, his head bowed and eyes shut. In shock, Kathryn dropped her knife, waiting for what was going to happen. It was as if Rafe expected to be beheaded and accepted it…even bowing his head for the blade.

The Admiral sheathed the cutlass in his belt, pulled his fist back and struck Rafe across the face. The blow knocked the boy to the ground. When he stood up to face his captain, Kathryn saw a trickle of blood running down the side of his jaw, most likely caused by one of the rings on the Admiral's fingers. He faced his leader, his face impassive and hard as stone.

"My command is not to be ignored for any reason, understand?" the Admiral spat.

"Aye, sir," Rafe answered.

"Good. Search her." The Admiral pointed in the direction of the girl. Rafe turned toward her, his fists clenched and his jaw set. He picked up the knife that she dropped. She cried out, backing away as his steps advanced toward her. He grabbed her arms, pinned her against a tree…then hesitated, looking towards his captain. Kathryn saw indecision flickering in his attractive blue eyes. Finally, he turned towards her.

"Do you have any more weapons?" he whispered. She shook her head. Suddenly, she tensed up as he bent quickly and ran his hands over her legs. He hastily pulled away and then turned to the Admiral. Kathryn's face was red with humiliation.

"Admiral!" a voice announced. George and three other guards came into view, holding up two men between them. "We have the prisoners you wanted,"

The Admiral walked over to them, peering into the face of Wilam and Halkins.

"Thank you, men," he said. "Leave them with me."

Setting the bound prisoners on the ground in front of the Admiral, George left with his guards. Kathryn tore away from Rafe's grip on her arms and ran over to Wilam.

"Wilam! You're alive," she whispered, kneeling beside him and brushing the sun bleached brown hair out of his eyes. Rafe's blue eyes narrowed when he saw Wilam lean his head slightly into Kathryn's touch.

Halkins groaned as he stood up to face the Admiral.

"We meet finally after all these years," Halkins said. The Admiral raised an eyebrow.

"I shall say the same, John Halkins," he said, "I hear you have been searching for me."

"Aye,"

"May I ask why?"

"To stop you from destroying New Harbour. You can't do this, Drake. You can't destroy the trade at the harbor like what you did to my family." Halkins set his jaw.

"Oh?" the Admiral laughed. "Who is going to stop me? You and what army? I am the most powerful man in the world right now, and though not everyone knows me, they will. They will when I become the all supreme ruler of the world with my black-sailed fleet!" the Admiral shouted. His voice lowered as he looked to Wilam.

"Stand up, Wilam," he said. Kathryn helped Wilam to stand and he faced the man. The Admiral peered into the boy's battered face. "You've changed."

"You haven't...Uncle," Wilam said. The Admiral cocked his head to the right, amused, then turned to Rafe.

"Take the girl to her quarters as I commanded earlier," the Admiral instructed.

"Aye, sir,"

Chapter Twenty-Two

"Come with me, Wilam, Halkins." The Admiral said after Rafe led Kathryn away. Wilam watched them until they were out of sight, narrowing his eyes with fury. His gut twisted with detestation as he saw Rafe place his hand around Kathryn's waist. Before they were completely out of sight down the path, Kathryn glanced up at Wilam, fear pulsing through her eyes.

Wilam turned and followed the Admiral and Halkins. They were led down the same road that the Admiral had taken Kathryn the night before. Shortly, they were led to the same view as Kathryn...overlooking the army of black ships.

Halkins' face contorted with rage as he saw the *Farrow* on her side, halfway stained the color black and stripped of her sails.

"How can you do this?" he snapped to the Admiral, who was twirling a pearl-handled pistol on his finger.

"The desire for control, order, and fear, my dear Halkins, rules all," he answered. "You are a proficient man, Halkins. If you also desire this, I will be able to offer you a place back on your ship as captain under my command." Halkins frowned inwardly. He was offered a place in the Admiral's army to rule the city he had wanted to save? Though he wanted the *Farrow* back. She was all he had left in the world. He loved his ship. Should he join?

The Admiral turned to Wilam.

"I have high hopes for you, my boy, if you also choose to join me again. We will forget the past, and you will become a powerful man. Perhaps even captain your own ship,"

Wilam simply stared at the fleet in awe and horror. He now realized what George had meant when they were in the carpenter's hall, trying to convince Wilam to join the mutiny. Each ship had their own captain, like Maldone was captain of one of the galleons. Wilam's uncle offered him a place as captain of one of the ships.

His uncle was the commanding officer, the admiral of the fleet.

Wilam swallowed. It was tempting. It was so tempting. He had wanted to be a captain of his own ship ever since he was a young boy. It was an opportunity of a lifetime for him. He would be powerful. He would be respected. No more beatings. No more stealing. He would have the respect of so many people.

But to captain a black sailed ship as part of an evil fleet…

The respect and awe would be out of fear.

Fear of him.

Wilam didn't know if he wanted that.

Suddenly, Wilam frowned. Who was *his* captain? The man he respected? Or the man he feared?

Wilam respected Halkins, but he feared his uncle, the Admiral. He would rather be like Halkins than his own uncle.

"To further educate you in my ways, let us go down to the harbor to witness the work done in my city. Shall we?" the Admiral unbound the men's wrists and gestured for them to go ahead of him down the path to the wharf.

Chapter Twenty-Three

Kathryn shrugged away from Rafe, walking faster down the path. She crossed her arms in front of her and kept her head down. She felt his hand on her shoulder.

"Miss Thatcher, stop," he said quietly. They were surrounded by trees that grew around the path, creating a sort of shady tunnel that sheltered them from the view of anyone. She didn't face him until Rafe's hand on her shoulder prompted her to turn around.

"Please, Rafe," she begged, meeting his blue eyes. "Leave me alone. You are loyal to your admiral; I'm just a prisoner."

"You are very beautiful," Rafe said, "My Admiral has pity on you because of it. That is why he has let you live so long."

"Does he not let women who come on the ships live?"

"Not always," Rafe looked around. They were alone. "Listen, I can help you get away from here."

"I am not leaving without my father," Kathryn announced. Rafe rolled his eyes back.

"Very well. I can help you get yourself and your father away from this island," Kathryn sensed he was lying.

"I thought you were strictly loyal to your Admiral."

"Aye…" he wavered.

"I saw his face when he…you…" she pointed to the dried blood on his jaw. "He almost killed you. How can you be loyal to a man like that?"

He grabbed her wrist, his head down. His eyes drifted up to meet her gaze. They were stony and hard.

"Who wouldn't fear him?" he whispered harshly. He touched two faint white scars on his face, which curved in perfect symmetry from the tip of his ear to halfway under his cheekbones. "I live in constant fear of everything around this island that surrounds him. You haven't seen what he will do to those who don't obey him, Miss Thatcher…"

She stared, helpless, at him, her wrist still in his forceful grip.

"Yet you didn't obey him earlier...Why would you want to help me?" she whispered. She stared at the scars. He didn't answer. All of a sudden, he dipped his face towards hers. Sensing what he was trying to do, she evaded his kiss and twisted out of his grip, backing off the path, away from him.

"Rafe, please," she exclaimed, stumbling backwards through the woods. He advanced towards her step by step until she cried out, turned, and ran through the brush as fast as her tired limbs could take her.

Chapter Twenty-Four

Wilam stared in awestruck wonder at the vast harbor that moored the black ships. He walked by the side of his uncle and Halkins past the stripped *Farrow* as she lay on her side; she was already painted halfway black. Her mast was fully repaired. The prisoners swarmed around the ship, painting, scraping off barnacles, repairing, and the like.

"Where are her sails?" Halkins asked the Admiral as they continued on.

"Ah. They are being dyed black, as the rest of my ships have black sails."

"Why the color black?" Wilam asked. The Admiral sighed and then turned to Wilam, rather exasperated.

"The color black is the color of death, evil, mystery, and fear, Wilam. It is what I want to be struck into the hearts of people when they see me in my splendor. I recall discussing this with you when you received my marking on your left shoulder blade. Am I correct?"

"Aye, sir," Wilam remembered. Painfully.

"May I see the tattoo, Nephew?"

It was more of a command than a question. Wilam turned around and pulled off his shirt without a word. The man's cold fingers traced his emblem proudly.

"Yes," the Admiral said quietly to himself. Wilam shuddered and pulled his shirt on once again, turning to face the man. The Admiral nodded once and began walking down the harbor, explaining the origins of ships and what kind of vessels they were.

"Do they have names?" Halkins asked.

"Nay. I only distinguish them by numbers. One, Two, Three, et cetera. They are simply known as the Black Sails as a whole. I do not bother with names."

The Admiral led them on. Soon, they came to a large galleon with three rows of oars.

"This beauty is my beloved. She is the leader of the rest and the one I most enjoy using for her power and speed. Although she is a galleon, I have had her situated with her three rows of oars to add speed for such a large ship. I actually have two galleons with three rows of oars. The other one is Maldone's. Nearly all of my…disagreeable prisoners row down below. As I have said before, I usually try to refrain from killing unless it is absolutely necessary. Otherwise, I send all of the difficult prisoners to the galleys."

"Is George a captain?" Wilam asked.

"No, my boy. George is a covert seaman whom I send to try to turn ship crews against their captains and take over the ships. With the *Farrow* he succeeded and he will be greatly rewarded."

"Sir?" Wilam stared at a gallows that was raised high above the harbor. A dead body swung from the rope, overlooking the dozens of ships and prisoners.

"This unfortunate man was caught setting fire to one of my frigates. He hangs there as a reminder to all of my slaves to beware of what they think would bring me to my ruin."

"Pardon me for saying this, sir, but suppose you were walking about like you are now, and someone tries to…to kill you?" Wilam asked, unflinchingly. The Admiral chuckled.

"How naïve you are, my boy. You don't realize, but I always have several private bodyguards who stay by me day and night while I am on the island. They are trained to stay hidden and alert,"

Wilam looked around uneasily. He saw nobody, save the slaves and slave masters, and multiple peasants. All of them seemed uninterested as they quickly walked about their tasks.

My uncle is not as brave as he appears to be, Wilam thought.

"It grows late. I want to request your presence at my residence to dine with my men and I. Do you accept, gentlemen?" the Admiral said, turning to Halkins and Wilam.

"Aye, sir," they said, nearly in unison.

"Excellent. We shall dine in one hour. Do you have anything you want to retrieve from your ship as we go back? Clothes? Weapons?"

"Aye, sir,"

"Then let us be off,"

Chapter Twenty-Five

Her breath came in ragged gasps as Kathryn fled through the trees. Suddenly she tripped on a root that stuck out from the ground in front of her. She stumbled to the earth. Tears sprung in her green eyes, blurring her vision, as she raised herself up to her feet once again. Blindly, she staggered through the brush. Her legs grew weak, and her steps faltered. A figure stepped out in front of her and she crashed into Rafe's chest. She cried out as he wrapped his arms around her, refusing to let her go. She kicked and screamed, but he held her relentlessly. Exhausted, Kathryn grew limp. She closed her eyes and inhaled deeply, trying to catch her breath. Her head leaned into Rafe's chest and she closed her eyes, gasping for air. She heard his heart beating.

"I love you," he said to her. He looked down to meet her eyes. "That's why I would help you escape from this island."

"No you don't," she retorted, refusing to meet his gaze. She tried once more, in vain, to break free from his grasp. "You don't love me. You don't know what love is. If you did, you would not handle me so forcefully. You wouldn't be so despicable. You don't know what love is!" She cried. She was close to tears.

"Do you?" he snorted, his grip tightening cruelly. She stopped. Did she know what love was?

"I…I…"

She felt his hand on the back of her head, prohibiting her from pulling away. Her whole body tensed up as he set his lips to hers coldly, kissing her hard on the mouth. He released her suddenly and she stumbled backwards, tears pouring down her cheeks.

"Go, Miss Thatcher," he growled and pointed into the forest. He stepped towards her and placed her knife that he had taken from her into her hand. "Disappear and do not let me see you again. It is better for you if you find a way to leave this island with or without your father. Go. I will not follow."

She ran.

He turned away, looking back only once, before walking back to the path. Inwardly, he grimaced. His Admiral would not be pleased that he had let the girl get away. Why had he? She wasn't worth anything to Rafe. She was just another prisoner. A beautiful prisoner, but still a prisoner. Rafe didn't want her to be killed by the Admiral and his plan he had for the girl. Rafe had only heard part of the plan, and it was not good.

He ran his hands through his hair and then sat down on the rough jungle floor.

What was happening to him? He actually let her get away. Why did he care about what happened to that little wretch?

He shook his head and stood up.

She was gone. He didn't have to deal with her anymore.

Kathryn ran until her legs gave way under her. She fell to the sandy floor of the forest, weeping. She would never get off of this horrible island. She would never rescue her father. Her father was weak and malnourished. He would not last another week under the conditions he was in now.

After a while, Kathryn grew silent. She pulled herself up to a sitting position and looked around. The trees were dense and birds flitted to and from branches. It was a pretty jungle.

A noise startled her. Someone was walking slowly towards her, taking careful, quiet steps. Kathryn crawled to the trunk of a tree and hid behind it, peeking out in the direction of the sound.

A girl walked into Kathryn's view. She was about thirteen, with long, wavy hair the color of golden honey. She was tall and slim, clothed in a navy blue dress with a baby blue apron. Her face was round, childish, and playful with dark brown eyes and long lashes around them. Humming, she swung a basket from her right elbow, looking up into the trees.

"Aha!" the girl exclaimed, and set down her basket. Kathryn glanced up to where the girl was looking and saw a bunch of yellow fruit. Bananas!

Kathryn's stomach rumbled and she felt weak. She had had no food since the hard bread last night. Shifting into a more comfortable position, she cringed when the brush crackled beneath her. The golden-haired girl stopped suddenly, peering towards Kathryn's hiding place.

Kathryn peeked out, guiltily.

"Hello," the girl said, coming closer. Kathryn stood up and faced the girl.

"Hello," Kathryn whispered. The girl looked Kathryn over. Kathryn suddenly felt tousled and disarrayed, ashamed of how unkempt she probably looked.

"I have never seen you before," the girl said, gently. "What's your name?"

"I…I'm Kathryn Thatcher," Kathryn answered, looking down at her bare feet and curling up her toes beneath them. "I came on the *Farrow* the other day when we were captured,"

"I'm Meg. I heard about the *Farrow*. Broken mast, right?"

"Aye…yes,"

"Are you all right? You look as if you've been crying," Meg said, compassionately. The way she so kindly said it was too much for Kathryn. She shook her head and began to cry. Meg reached over and embraced

Kathryn tenderly. Kathryn cried into Meg's shoulder, grateful for a friend.

"Kathryn Thatcher," Meg said as soon as Kathryn had calmed down once again. She took Kathryn's shoulders and led her through the forest. "Come with me. Tell me everything,"

Chapter Twenty-Six

Wilam stood in front of the mirror, staring into his transformed reflection. He had retrieved his satchel of belongings from the *Farrow* and had changed into his nice clothes. He wore a white cotton shirt and black vest over new trousers, a red scarf for a belt, and boots. His sandy brown hair was washed and combed back, tied in a short braid with a red ribbon. He touched his freshly shaved jaw and adjusted his cottony vest.

He sighed and then turned to leave, when his eyes fell on the leather satchel that rested on the dresser. Slowly, he picked it up and touched the worn stitches. The smell of musty beaten leather wafted up to his nose.

It was Kathryn's.

She had dropped it when George on the *Farrow* found them out and hauled them on deck. Wilam had seen it after he had retrieved his satchel from his quarters and picked it up, hiding it with his other bag.

With slender fingers, he unhooked the clasp and reached inside. He pulled out a worn red book that he recognized instantly from the ship: Kathryn's book of poetry.

Wilam flipped through it, the words meaning nothing to his illiterate eyes. He set it down and pulled out another book from in the satchel. This one was smaller and tattered by many hours of being held.

He flipped through this book too, also unable to read the words written in there by Kathryn's hand. Suddenly, he turned back a few pages and stopped. There, drawn with charcoal, was a portrait of a young man. Wilam stared, looked into the mirror, and then looked back at the image in the notebook. It was him. It was a picture of Wilam Eugene, drawn there as plain as day.

He choked, stifling a gasp.

"She drew me," he whispered, clutching the book tightly. He flipped through the rest of the pages, looking for any other drawing she might have done. There wasn't any more, other than a sketch of a bunch of daisies.

Wilam looked through the rest of the satchel. There were several thin pieces of charcoal and at the very bottom was a small, golden chain. He pulled it out, brushed charcoal dust from it, and observed it. The light glinted off of the necklace and the pendant that dangled from it was a simple, tiny, beautifully crafted golden leaf.

"Wilam?" a voice called from in the hallway. Quickly, Wilam thrust the journal and the necklace into his pocket and turned to see John Halkins approaching his doorway. He was dressed sharply in his captain's attire from the *Farrow*, with a long blue coat and shiny boots. His hair and beard were sleek and trimmed.

"Good day, Captain Halkins," Wilam greeted. Halkins nodded.

"Good day, Wilam," he replied, then whispered, "Be careful about addressing me as captain, boy. I don't know what the Admiral would think. You know what I mean?"

"Aye,"

"You look dashing tonight," Halkins changed the subject, looking Wilam over.

"As do you, sir." Wilam paused.

“What is it, son?” Halkins asked, his voice dropping to a low whisper. He noticed Wilam’s tentativeness.

“I don’t know what to do, Cap,” Wilam sighed. “What if I get to captain a ship? Should I accept it? I really don’t want to. What are you going to do?”

“If I get the opportunity?”

“Aye, sir.”

“I’d accept. But I would do my best to destroy the man and his plans.”

“But what do I do?”

“Whatever you think is best.” Halkins said, “You’re worried about something else,”

“Aye, sir. Kathryn.” Wilam said after a moment.

“I don’t know what we can do, Will,” Halkins said finally. He sighed, and then looked out into the hall. “Shall we go to the dining room? I believe I hear some company.”

The men walked through the grand, massive hallways of the Admiral’s residence, finding their way to the dining room. When they located it, they went through the open doors. Men in fine captain’s attire milled about in the room, talking and enjoying themselves. Wilam noticed Edmund Maldone, the pale captain who had captured the *Farrow*, in the midst of the men. In the middle of the room, a large table sat, big enough to seat about forty people.

"Remember, Wilam," Halkins whispered to the boy, "Play like you're loyal and all in. Got it?"

Wilam nodded.

The Admiral came over to Halkins and Wilam and greeted them. He led them to their seats at either side of the seat at the head of the table. He took his place at the head and raised his hands. The men all went to their seats and sat down.

"Attention, gentlemen," he said in a loud voice. The room became quiet. "I want to thank you all for joining me, your Admiral Henry Drake, for dinner tonight. As you all are probably aware, the arrival of the *Farrow* institutes the fortieth ship in my fleet."

The men applauded. Wilam glanced over at Halkins, astounded by the number. Forty ships in five years…

"I would also like to introduce John Halkins, who will resume his captainship of the former *Farrow* as captain of Number *Forty*. That is, if he chooses to join and accept the duty and command under my control."

Halkins had stood up as his name was said. He faced the Admiral.

"John Halkins, do you accept this title as captain of Number *Forty*?"

The room was still, anticipating Halkins' answer.

"Aye, Admiral. I accept with great pleasure."

The room erupted in cheers and congratulations as the Admiral smiled arrogantly and pinned on a black crest medal onto his new comrade's chest. The food came and was set in front of the men by uniformed servants. Wilam now realized why all of the men looked so healthy and strong. They ate like kings! Fruit and meat filled the table and ale, whiskey, brandy, and wine flowed freely.

"You all also realize the tragedy that has befallen the disloyal captain of Number *Twenty-Three*. Theodore Sterne attempted to destroy his ship with fire, costing us days to repair. He was severely and…permanently…punished. This has left us with an able ship with no captain. Therefore, I propose my returned nephew, Wilam Eugene Drake, to captain the ship in Sterne's place. Do I hear aye or nay?" The

Admiral gestured to Wilam, who stood up as he was introduced.

“I say nay,” A pale, pallid man in a black coat stood up, pushing his chair back as he stood.

“Edmund Maldone. Explain your denial,”

“With pleasure, Admiral Drake. Look at him!” Maldone pointed to the young man and all eyes turned to Wilam. He felt the tips of his ears heat up in discomfiture. “Sir; gentlemen: He is naught but eighteen, are you, boy?”

“I will be eighteen in a month, sir,” Wilam replied.

“Only seventeen and given the opportunity to captain a ship with very little experience. There are plenty of other able and loyal men who can take his place. This is my argument, Admiral,” Maldone resumed his seat and crossed his arms.

“I hear your objection,” The Admiral replied. “However, Wilam was born and raised on a ship and knows the qualifications of a captain. Understanding your agitation, I will appoint an assistant captain to Wilam, if he chooses to accept the captain’s position. Does that arrangement suit well?”

“Aye,” Maldone answered, sulkily.

"Are there any more objections?" the Admiral asked, looking around the room. No one opposed. He turned to Wilam. "Do you accept the position of a captain on ship Number *Twenty-Three*?"

"Aye, sir. It is an honor," Wilam answered. The Admiral draped a black captain's coat over the boy, and then placed the captain's black crest onto the chest of it. Applause filled the room as Wilam Eugene Drake became the youngest captain in the Black Sailed fleet.

Chapter Twenty-Seven

As night settled over the island, Meg, her mother Anna, and Meg's little sister Claire, ate slowly, watching Kathryn as she gulped down the food placed in front of her.

"I cannot believe you came all the way from New Harbour without an escort, just to find your father," Anna said, in shock. Kathryn had just finished telling her and Meg everything that had happened since she left her city. For some reason, however, she was afraid to mention Rafe.

"I don't believe it either…but I felt that I had to. My papa is the only family that I have left, and I don't think he will live much longer," Kathryn said softly. She glanced at little Claire, and then stroked the girl's light red hair. She was about five with wide, blue eyes and a smile that boasted missing teeth.

"Have you met the Admiral?" Meg asked, sipping her tea.

"Aye…I mean, yes, I did. He's horrible. Every time I was brought near the man, I felt chills." Kathryn sighed. "I don't think it was worth coming all the way here to find Papa. This island is filled with evil and I don't know how I will ever get back, with or without Papa."

"You regret coming?" Anna asked.

"Sometimes. It all seems so hopeless." Kathryn stopped talking. She swallowed the lump in her throat and blinked back hot tears that seared her eyelids. Meg spoke up to try to relieve the tension and awkwardness.

"Mama and I have been on this island all of our lives," Meg said. "The Admiral came about five years ago and took it over because he liked the location and size of the island. We used to be a small village, but he turned it into his own city. None of us could leave, even if we wanted to, because he took our only two ships for his fleet."

"So I will never get back to New Harbour?" Kathryn asked.

"Well..." Anna said as she and Meg looked at one another. Claire played in the corner with a little cloth doll, oblivious to the conversation that was taking place.

"There has been talk...rumors...about the fleet," Meg whispered, leaning over the table towards Kathryn.

"What kind of rumors?"

"The number of the ships has reached forty, counting the *Farrow*. People are wondering if his fleet is complete, and if he is going to launch his attack on New Harbour soon,"

"Isn't that bad?" Kathryn was confused at Meg's eagerness. Meg shook her honey curls and grinned.

"Not all of it. See, the Admiral appoints captains of his ships, according to men he believes are worthy and loyal to him. What he doesn't realize is that not all of the captains plan to comply with all of his commands. They've started a secret rebellion against the Admiral. Nearly twenty captains and crews we know of are in it already."

"And?"

"And, whenever the fleet is released to conquer New Harbour, the Admiral will go down and the prisoners and captives will be released from his tyranny!"

"How do you know all this?" Kathryn asked, stunned. Hope was beginning to sprout once again in her being.

"My papa is a captain," Meg explained, shrugging. "Why do you think we get these nice accommodations?" she gestured around the small house.

"He is part of the rebellion?"

"Yes…" Meg whispered. "So many people hate the Admiral, but are too afraid of him to show it. He has terrible punishments…"

"That's enough, Margaret," Anna said.

"Yes, Mama. But, Kathryn, think of it! We could be rid of him. It all depends on how soon he decides to conquer New Harbour."

Kathryn stared at her and then smiled. Her father had a chance to be rescued from the Admiral and his horrendous oars.

"Why are you waiting? Why not rebel now?" she inquired.

"We can't," explained Anna, "The Admiral is guarded by several guards and cannot be killed or approached. He keeps an eye on his captains. He also has all of the civilians, like us, watched constantly. We live in fear. When the ships are launched out on the sea for the attack, it will be near impossible for the Admiral to know what is going on among his fleet. That is why the rebel captains must remain 'loyal' to the Admiral on the island, so he doesn't suspect. Then they can rebel on the sea and he can't do anything about it."

"Why are you telling me this?" Kathryn asked. "Why do you trust me?"

"Something tells me that we can trust you." Anna said, a twinkle in her eye.

"What? What tells you that?"

"Kathryn, you have had a long day. We can talk more tomorrow."

"I don't want to impose," Kathryn stood up. She didn't want to take advantage of the family's kindness.

"No, Kathryn. You are welcome to stay as long as you need. Meg, you and Kathryn go get cleaned up and get your bed ready. Kathryn, dear, you may have those two dresses on the door and the nightgown and apron, also," Anna pointed to the dresses that hung on the hook of the door. Kathryn shook her head.

"No, no. Those are Meg's!"

“I outgrew those last year, Kathryn.” Meg said, laughing. “See, I'm taller than you are…though, you're older.” she compared herself to Kathryn.

“They are so pretty…” Kathryn touched the fabric reverently. Indeed they were. One was a dark, navy blue with long sleeves and white collar and sash. The other was green trimmed with darker emerald around the sleeves and hem. A brown apron hung up with them. “Thank you, so much,” Kathryn said, turning to Anna and Meg. Anna gathered a tired Claire in her arms and took her to her bed.

Later, clothed in their nightgowns, the girls sat on Meg’s bed. Meg ran her bristle comb through Kathryn’s long, dark hair, removing all the tangles.

“You have such a good family.” Kathryn said, rather wistfully. Meg was silent for a moment.

“Do…do you have any other family besides your father?” she asked gently.

“No,” Kathryn gave a small laugh, “My mother died when I was a baby. Papa raised me, but he was gone most of the time for ship business. I saw him about once a week. Until I was eleven, I lived with an old neighbor woman who cared for me while Papa was away. She was old and blind, so it was I caring for her most of the time. Then she died when I was almost eleven. Papa took me on a ship to New Harbour because he wanted to raise me properly on a small farm he had his eye on. He even spoke of getting remarried…" Kathryn bit her lip at the memory.

"Did you have friends?" Meg asked.

"Almost," Kathryn said softly. She turned away from Meg and burrowed into the coverlets. She did not want to talk about her early life anymore.

It was a few hours until she fell asleep.

When she finally did, the silver moonlight shone on her serene face that was wet with tears.

Chapter Twenty-Eight

"Men, it has been five years since the beginning of my quest to complete my fleet," The Admiral said to the captains around the dining table. The dishes were cleared away and the men turned their attention to the Admiral and his speech he was about to make. "In that time, I have achieved thirty-nine new ships to be in my convoy other than my galleon. You, men, are my captains and loyal followers. You all are aware of the plan to take control of New Harbour, and that plan is about to come to life! In three days, we will go out to accomplish that mission,"

The room erupted in cheers.

Wilam cringed inwardly. He didn't want to do this. He felt no loyalty to the man beside him and felt too young to captain a pirate's ship, killing and commanding under that man's rule.

“A drink,” the Admiral lifted up a glass of ale, and the men did likewise. Wilam didn’t touch his. “A toast to the defeat of New Harbour!”

“Aye!” a chorus of joie de vivre and high spirits filled the room as the men drank. Wilam felt nauseous and sick to his stomach. He stood from his chair, unnoticed.

“I'm going to step outside a moment,” he whispered to Halkins, who looked as if he wanted to join Wilam, but decided to go along with his façade of being a loyal captain to the Admiral.

Wilam wove in between the bustling crowd of men who were drinking and getting second rounds of ale and brandy. He slipped out of the door and onto the torch lit veranda.

The sun was setting and night was settling over the city. The air around Wilam was cool, and he adjusted the black coat around his upper body. It was a beautiful garment, a genuine piece of captain’s attire. He leaned against the railing and sighed, hating himself.

He didn’t want to be a captain. He wasn’t ready for this. He was a coward for not refusing. He would disappoint his new crew and they would resent him for his higher ranking at his young age. He would have to be loyal to his evil uncle and obey all of his commands without question. He would have to obey his uncle in everything…including murdering if that was what was required of him.

His thoughts drifted to Kathryn. He reached into his pocket, withdrawing the golden necklace. He gazed at the small, intricate, golden leaf nestling in his palm.

"Where are you?" he whispered, looking out to the harbor where he could barely make out the masts of the ships.

If he were to be a captain, he could request that Kathryn be on his ship…if he could find her. He could steal her away and hide her in the hold if need be.

"Hail…Captain," a voice sneered mockingly at him from the shadows. Wilam slipped the necklace into his pocket once again.

"Who's there?" Wilam squinted, peering into the darkness, trying to make out the owner of the voice. A young man, about the same age as Wilam, revealed himself and joined Wilam at the railing. He was tall and blonde. Wilam thought he looked familiar, but couldn't place his finger on *why*.

"Rafe Norrington," the blonde said, narrowing his blue eyes. Wilam inhaled sharply as he remembered the lad. It was the same guard who had led Kathryn away earlier that afternoon.

"You," Wilam growled.

"Did you get offered a position as captain, *Wilam Drake*?" Rafe asked coldly, eyeing the black coat and captain's crest.

"So what if I did?" Wilam suddenly grabbed Rafe by his shirt and slammed him against the wall. "Where's Kathryn?"

Rafe remained silent. Wilam opened his mouth to ask again, but Rafe reared back a clenched fist and smashed it into Wilam's face. Wilam cried out in pain and rage, dropping Rafe. The blonde took advantage of Wilam's injured diversion and wrapped his meaty arm around Wilam's neck, choking him. Wilam gasped for air, his nose spilling blood from the punch he had received, before reaching his hands behind his head and grabbing one of Rafe's arms. He twisted forward sharply, and Rafe crashed to the ground. He leaped onto Rafe, punching him twice in the face until Rafe rolled over so that he was on top and Wilam's head knocked to the floor. His elbow crashed into Wilam's ear, flipping him over to his side. White spots danced in front of Wilam's eyes. Enraged, Wilam crouched as Rafe loomed behind him, suddenly rearing up and swinging his fist into Rafe's jaw. Rafe staggered back as Wilam pounced again, kicked the boy over, and pinned him to the ground.

Both young men breathed heavily, Rafe heaving under Wilam with his wrists pinned to the ground. Sweat and blood trickled from both faces.

"Where is Kathryn?" Wilam repeated. The light from the torch flickered on his sweaty, wounded face.

"How should I know?" Rafe spat furiously. Wilam slammed Rafe's head into the boardwalk, causing the blonde to wince.

"Where is she?" Wilam rasped.

"She ran off into the forest. I haven't seen her since this afternoon."

"What did you do to her?"

"Nothing," Rafe hesitated. Wilam reared back his fist, ready to strike him again. The teenager flinched and turned his face away.

"What did you do?" Wilam repeated in a low voice.

"I kissed her," Rafe snarled spitefully through clenched teeth. Wilam's stomach twisted and a roar exploded from his throat as he struck Rafe's face one last time. He moaned and lay still.

"Get up," Wilam snapped, getting off of Rafe. As he stood, Wilam slammed him into the wall again and spat at the boy. "Where is she, really?"

"I told you, she ran off into the forest. I…I let her go," Rafe stammered, wiping his battered cheek with his sleeve.

"You let her go." Wilam scoffed, not believing him.

"Aye, the Admiral was going to kill her,"

"Explain yourself."

"He was talking about sending her to the galleys with her father. She'll die in less than three days if she's sent down there."

"Why is he sending her there?" Wilam questioned through clenched teeth.

"He said that she knows too much." Rafe rolled his eyes to the back of his head. "He's going to kill me for letting her go…"

"Oh, how I want to be the one to do that right now..." Wilam said, cynically. "What are you doing here?"

"Dunno," he shrugged. Rafe pressed the back of his hand to his eye, the skin around it throbbing as it began to bruise. Wilam shoved the boy off the veranda; he stumbled onto the grass.

"Get out of here, Rafe. Now!" Wilam shouted as the blonde began to run down the path into the darkness. "Stay away from Kathryn, or I will kill you!"

Chapter Twenty-Nine

The morning was hazy and gloomy as Kathryn stepped downstairs into the breakfast room. Meg and her mother sat at the table, eating, and a man was with them. Claire was perched on his knee, giggling.

"Good morning, Kathryn!" Meg said, cheerily. She jumped up and began to serve a plate for their guest. Kathryn sat down in the chair, accepting the plate with thanks. "This is my papa," Meg said, gesturing to the man as she sat down.

"Good day, Miss Kathryn," the man said, smiling. "My name is Charles."

Kathryn returned the smile. She liked this man. His eyes were a warm brown, surrounded by wrinkles from smiling. Claire pulled on his reddish beard gently.

"Good day, Charles," she said, and shook his hand.

"Papa was telling us about the meeting last night," Meg explained.

"What meeting?" Kathryn asked Charles, taking a bite out of her warm, soft bread. Charles glanced at Anna.

"Does she know?" he mouthed. Anna nodded, and he turned to Kathryn. "You know that I am a captain in the fleet, and that I am part of the…rebellion,"

"Yes, sir," Kathryn replied.

"The Admiral had a meeting last night with all of his captains. There are now forty ships in his fleet, and he is ready to take over New Harbour. It is about time for us to rise up against him and destroy him,"

"When is he planning on the attack?" Anna asked her husband.

"He said in three days," Charles answered.

"Three days!" Meg exclaimed. Kathryn's eyes went wide. Only three days…

"Also, listen to this," Charles leaned forward over the table and whispered: "You know Sterne's ship, the cap'n who was hanged?"

The women nodded, listening closely.

"Well, he chose a cap'n in his place. A seventeen-year-old boy,"

"No!" Anna said, appalled. "Why?"

"It's his nephew, he said," Charles supposed. Kathryn drew in her breath sharply. *Wilam.* It could only be Wilam!

"What ship does he captain?" she asked, trying to sound calm. Her heart was beating wildly. It hurt to breathe.

"*Twenty-Three*, I believe…"

"What's his name?" Kathryn asked.

"William…I think. It was an unusual sort of name like that

…Odd…"

"Wilam?"

"That's it,"

"So old Drake has a nephew?" Meg asked, dismayed.

"Apparently so," said Charles, laughing, "He's probably just like the old admiral. I watched him a bit last night, but he left early, so I didn't get to talk to him. He seemed a bit overwhelmed."

"Seventeen…" Anna leaned back in her chair, shaking her graying blonde head.

"Where did he come from?" Meg asked. "I don't ever remember the Admiral having a nephew."

Charles shrugged. Kathryn bit her lip, wondering if she should tell her hosts that she knew the boy.

"It's despicable," Anna said, scornfully. "I don't see how he could do that. And Sterne was a good man. He was just impulsive, that's all,"

"Well, the boy seems inexperienced. He should be easy to take down." Charles began to rise from his seat.

"No!" Kathryn blurted. The family looked at her, surprised. "Wilam is a good man. He…he was kind to me on the *Farrow*."

"He was on the ship with you?" Anna asked.

"Yes…I met him on that ship. He was a sails man, and he had been at sea his whole life. He was my…escort. He made sure that I was safe, even though I didn't think that I needed him." Kathryn looked down at her empty plate.

"Did you know he was the Admiral's nephew?" Charles asked the girl. She shook her head, flushing in spite of herself. She saw the look exchanged between Charles and Anna. Did they trust her?

"Not until the day that we were captured by one of the captains," she said, adding: "He told me…and he is not on his uncle's side. He wants to destroy him."

"Ah," Charles said.

"Why is everyone talking so much?" Claire asked, her missing teeth causing her to speak with a lisp. Everyone laughed, relieved to break the tension.

"Fascinating," Charles stood and pushed his chair back into the table. He stepped to the old bookshelf in the corner and pulled down a huge book.

"What is that?" asked Kathryn.

"A Bible," Meg said, looking shocked. "Don't you read the Bible?"

"No," Kathryn shrugged. She was curious.

Charles smiled, and then turned the thin, fragile pages to a place near the end of the massive book.

"Well, then, my dear," Charles said. "You are in for a pleasure."

He cleared his throat, and began to read.

"'This then is the message from which we have heard of and declare unto you, that God is light and in him is no darkness at all.'"

"What does that mean?" asked Kathryn, bewildered. What did it mean, no darkness? Nothing was without darkness. All her life had been was darkness. She had no hope left in her being to have even a little light.

"This verse talks about light and dark in the sense that light is goodness, and darkness is evil. It is sin. Everything in this world is sinful. The world is lost in darkness."

"That's terrible," Kathryn said and fell silent. *And yet so true.*

"Indeed, my dear. It is terrible. But, there is hope. God offers eternal light in a dark and sinful world."

"What light? What hope? There is no hope left," Kathryn whispered.

"God's light comes from a long time ago, when the world was just beginning. It was perfect until humans came and sinned, casting the rest of the world in darkness. Years and years passed. God saw that the world had lost hope. There was no hope for such a fallen life we lived. So, God decided to send part of Himself to the world in the form of a human…Jesus."

"Is this all true?" Kathryn asked doubtfully. Suddenly, her mind brought her the memory of when she was up in the crow's nest. She had felt a comforting presence as she stared at the stars. Was that God? In her mind, she doubted...but deep in her heart...she knew. She knew it was true.

"Every word,"

"What did Jesus do?"

Charles flipped some pages in the Bible and placed his finger on the worn words.

"'John 3:16: For God so loved the world that He sent His only begotten Son that whosoever believeth in Him shall not perish, but shall have everlasting life.'" Charles read. He looked at Kathryn, whose green eyes had a new glow in them. They were brighter with the thought of new hope. "God sent Jesus to come into the world and die for the sins that we committed. He died so the darkness of the world could have light."

"Wait!" Kathryn stood. "Jesus died? After all that, He died? What about the promise of eternal life?"

"This is the best part, Kathryn. Jesus conquered death because He is more powerful than death. He rose from the grave and is now waiting for you to believe in Him and live with Him eternally. He wants you to have His light."

"All I have to do is believe in Jesus?"

"Yes, and all that He did for you. You will forever have hope and joy, and darkness will no longer rule you."

Kathryn was silent.

"Do you believe this, Kathryn?" Charles asked. She pondered this, fiddled with her dress, and then stood up.

"I…I don't know." She said finally. This idea was odd. It scared her somewhat. Why would God want her? She was a nobody. She wasn't good enough. She refused to talk about it anymore. However, her mind was swirling with all the new promises of hope and joy. It sounded all too good. It sounded strange and wonderful. She wasn't sure.

"Lord we thank you for this new day. We thank you for bringing Miss Kathryn here to us. Bless her, Lord, and help her find what she is looking for…Help us defeat the Admiral…" Charles murmured.

Kathryn walked out of the room, suddenly afraid of the family's odd ways and beliefs.

Chapter Thirty

Wilam splashed cold water on his face, trying to wake up. He winced as he touched the purplish bruise on his jaw, reminding him of last night. His throat tightened. He had to find Kathryn today before anybody else did…specifically Rafe Norrington.

He cursed under his breath, shrugging the black captain's coat over his body. He hated Rafe for what he had done to Kathryn. If he ever saw the boy again, he swore that he would make him pay…more than he had last night.

Wilam sighed, straightening his coat. A knock on the door broke through his thoughts and he looked in the mirror to see his uncle standing in the doorway. Wilam's fist clenched.

"Wilam Eugene Drake," the Admiral greeted, coming closer to the boy.

"Uncle," he answered, curtly.

"Where have you been all these years?" the man asked. Wilam turned from the mirror to face him.

"I thought you said we would forget the past if I joined your fleet and swore loyalty to you,"

"Ah," the Admiral smiled a cold smile. "I did. But it does not satisfy my curiosity."

"Your curiosity does not abide well with me. I prefer to keep my past confidential for it would not interest you in the least." Wilam said haughtily. The Admiral raised an eyebrow.

"I see." The man replied. "Then, pray tell me, why did you run away from me? You could have been commanding a long time ago…"

"I hated you,"

"Do you still hate me, Wilam?" the Admiral asked. Wilam hesitated. Saying yes would spell disloyalty and saying no would be a complete lie.

"I…I don't know," he said finally.

"You don't know?"

Wilam remained silent.

"I see," the Admiral said again. He turned, about to leave the room, and placed his hand on the doorframe.

He didn't look at Wilam as he said: "Don't even try to destroy my ships. I know about the captains who think that they will bring me down, but they *will not* succeed. Do I make myself clear?"

"Why do you think you can do this?" Wilam burst out at his uncle. The man turned and looked at the boy, anger mounting in his face.

"I want people to fear me, to dread my very existence, to look up to me and obey my every command. I want to be an admiral that takes control and holds power over people with terror. I want to have the entire merchant line and harbor, the lord of trade! I have desired this my whole life and it is about to happen. No one will stand in my way. No one!" the Admiral yelled back at his nephew, seething and furious. "Get down to the harbor and ready your crew. Stock up on the weaponry and ammunition. George will be your first mate. Good day." He turned and slammed the door behind him. Wilam could hear his footsteps retreating down the marble hallway.

Wilam squared his shoulders, and walked out of his room, ready for his first day of captaining a ship. Two pistols and a cutlass were at his side, and a dagger went into each boot. He set out to the harbor, a determined look settled over his young face.

Chapter Thirty-One

Kathryn walked down the cobbled streets with Meg and Anna, the sun already hot as its rays beat down on the women's heads. Claire had been left at a trusted friend's home. Kathryn was told that the women were required to help load up the ships. All villagers helped in whatever way they were considered necessary, whether they wanted to or not. It was a command from the Admiral in preparation for the attack.

People bustled around, busy preparing the ships. Kathryn looked around, furtively hoping to catch a glimpse of Wilam. The women passed by a group of men who were staining a topsail of a ship. Black pitch was everywhere, and the men were also stained black. They were prisoners, with a man brandishing a whip overseeing them.

A few men were over to the side, patching the tears and rips in a dry sail. Kathryn looked closer at one man.

"Jack?" she cried, and then broke into a run. Jack looked up at the sound of his name and smiled when he saw Kathryn.

"Careful, Miss Kathryn," he laughed, holding up a black hand and forearm. She slowed down as she approached him. "I seem to be a bit soiled."

She laughed at his small joke and then looked at him closer. He was pale and unkempt, his black hair hanging in dirty strands over his eyes. His legs were stained black up to his knees and his arms were black up to his elbows. He had a bruise on his jaw and his lip was split as if he had been in a fight. Scratches marred his cheek.

"Are you all right, Jack?"

"Aye, never better…" he said, his smile faltering. "Don't worry about me, Miss Kathryn. I'm fine."

Kathryn jumped as a whip snapped in the air.

"Get to work, men!" the overseer barked. Jack bent over his sail, stitching the needle through the rough cloth.

"Go on, Miss," Jack whispered, "I don't want you to get in trouble."

Kathryn backed away and joined Meg and Anna, who had watched from a few meters away.

"He was Wilam's best friend on the *Farrow*," she explained simply.

"Come on girls," Anna said, walking faster down the streets. She looked anxious. "We need to find Papa's ship and help there,"

"What ship does your papa captain?" Kathryn asked Meg.

"Number *Eighteen*. I've only been down to the ship harbor a few times. It is normally too dangerous,"

"It still is. Stay near to me," Anna warned. The girls fell into step with Meg's mother. "I think the ships are in numerical order." she muttered, searching. Bustling crowds swarmed the harbor, proving difficult for the women to walk through. All of the black ships looked the same to Kathryn. However, on each of their black bows, their number name was painted boldly in red paint.

Twelve

Four

Thirty-Two

“Well,” Anna sighed, looking discouraged. The women walked and pushed through the masses with no luck finding *Eighteen*. “I suppose they are *not* in order…”

As they passed one ship, though, Kathryn’s ears perked up when she heard whispers.

“Is that the new captain?”

“He is so young!”

“And awfully dashing in his captain’s coat.”

“But handsome! Look at his jaw line…”

There was a round of giggling, and Kathryn saw who were talking. Several girls were pausing by the ship *Twenty-Three* on their way about their tasks. Kathryn tugged on Anna’s sleeve, and then pushed her way to the front of the crowd of females.

Wilam stood on the gangplank, ordering his crew as they loaded boxes and barrels and supplies into the ship. He was totally oblivious to the many female admirers on the harbor, who were gawking at him openly.

Kathryn also stared at him. He wore a black captain’s coat and was in full captain’s attire. His face was different, somehow. His jaw was set and hard, a resolute shine in his hazel brown eyes.

"Is that him?" Meg, who had appeared at her friend's side, murmured to Kathryn. "He's handsome," Kathryn could only nod. She was speechless. The throng of girls had thinned considerably when the overseers snapped at them to get back to their duties. Kathryn paid them no heed as she stood with Anna and Meg in front of the ship. Finally, Wilam glanced up. It was a moment before his eye caught Kathryn's.

"Kathryn?" he said, incredulously. The supervisor of the docks yelled at the women to get a move on, and Anna and Meg had to obey.

"Papa's ship is three over if you need us," Anna whispered and gave Kathryn's hand a squeeze.

"Thank you so much," Kathryn said to her. Meg and Anna left down the street.

Wilam said something to a burly man beside him and then ran off of the gangplank towards Kathryn. She held her arms out, smiling, and he embraced her warmly.

"Kathryn, Kathryn, Kathryn," he repeated, holding her close. She sighed and rested her head on his broad shoulder. After a moment, he pulled her away and looked into her eyes.

"Are you all right?" he asked her. She nodded.

"Yes. I've been staying with a family. They are very kind to me," she said.

"Did Rafe hurt you in any way?" Wilam blurted. Kathryn bit her lip and shifted her gaze away from him.

"N-no…" she faltered.

"He kissed you," Wilam said. She snapped her eyes back to him.

"How…how do you know that?"

"I beat it out of that rapscallion lout last night," Wilam fumed.

"He didn't hurt me," she said. His face softened as he looked at Kathryn once again. She touched the lapel of his black coat.

"So you really are a captain," she murmured.

"Aye," he took her hand gently. Suddenly, his expression changed, and he looked around. "Come with me. Quickly, now."

"What…" Kathryn started. Wilam shushed her and pulled her up the gangplank into his black ship. They passed the burly man on the deck and he looked at the two.

"George, make sure the ship is loaded. Take over for me," Wilam commanded the man.

"Aye, sir," George replied sarcastically, loathing to obey orders from Wilam. Men wove around them, loading the ship, repairing the ratlines, and the like. Wilam led Kathryn across the black deck and down to the captain's quarters. He tugged her into the room and shut the door behind her.

"Wilam, what is this all about?" she asked warily.

"It's about what Rafe told me last night," Wilam turned and opened the glass window, leaning on the davenport that rested underneath the window.

"What? What did he tell you?"

"He said that he let you go because the Admiral was going to send you to the galleys with your father,"

"To the galleys?" she exclaimed. Wilam nodded gravely.

"I feared for you. You wouldn't survive longer than three days,"

"What's going to happen now?" Kathryn moaned. She absentmindedly fiddled with her long dark braid.

"I don't know!" Wilam shouted. He ran his fingers through his hair. He turned away from her. "I don't know…"

"Wilam," Kathryn said in a soft voice, "I'm sorry. I wasn't trying to make you angry,"

"No...I'm sorry. I'm not angry..." Wilam bit his lip and faced her. She looked at him timidly. "I'm just...scared,"

"So am I," she whispered. "Why are you? You have everything. A ship. A captain's title. Riches. Freedom. You've always wanted that,"

"None of it matters anymore, Kathryn. I'm scared because...I can't do this alone. I can't take upon myself all the responsibility. I don't know what my uncle will do. He already wants to be rid of you. What will he do when he finds that you are on my ship? I'm terrified..."

"You don't have to do this alone. I can stay by your side. We can fight him together, Wilam." She pleaded. He shook his head.

"I want you out of harm's way. I'll keep you hidden here on my ship until we get to New Harbour,"

"But what about Papa, and Jack?"

"I...I can try to get your father. I don't know where Jack is..."

"But I saw him but a moment ago, patching the sails!"

"Patching the sails?"

"Yes, just up the path a ways. I stopped to talk to him. Oh, Wilam, he looks awful!"

"I'll go and get him. Being a captain does have its advantages," he grinned, and then turned to the door. He opened it halfway and glanced towards Kathryn. "I'll also find your father and bring him on my ship."

"And I will go with you," she said. She started to follow him. He stopped her.

"No. You are staying in here. I don't want to lose you again,"

"You won't lose me again," she said.

"You don't know that. I don't know that. I want you safe. You will stay in here." He said, guiltily realizing the commanding tone of his voice. Kathryn noticed the key gripped in his hand.

"You won't lock me in this room!" she said. Anger flickered in her eyes. Wilam shook his head and stepped out of the room.

"I will come and get you when I have your father and Jack." He shut the door behind him and turned the key.

"You are not my captain, Wilam!" he cringed, hearing her shout as he walked away down the hallway.

Chapter Thirty-Two

Wilam walked briskly down the street, holding his head up proudly like a captain should. Inside, though, he felt torn. He had not planned on locking Kathryn in the room, but he felt that was the only way to keep her safe from the Admiral and his threats. He suddenly grimaced.

He had forgotten to give her the necklace and journal.

He thought about going back to the ship, but he was already halfway up the road from it. He decided to give it to her when he got back.

Wilam looked all up and down the bustling streets for the sails men. He still remained unaware of the stares and whispers of fear that were going on around him as he passed the people on the streets.

In time, Wilam located the sail makers and their overseer. Jack looked up, surprised to see his old friend.

Even more surprised was he to see his old friend in captain's apparel.

Wilam went up to the overseer, without even acknowledging Jack, and spoke to the man.

Minutes later, Wilam led Jack roughly off as a bought and bound prisoner. Once out of sight of the overseer, Wilam swiftly untied Jack.

"Will!" Jack said, relieved. Wilam grinned, and the two friends embraced.

"Good to see you, Jack," Wilam said. He peered into Jack's bruised and cut face. "Although, you really don't look too good…"

"So what's with the captain costume?" Jack asked as the men started walking towards the ship.

"I actually am a captain, Jack," Wilam began to explain all about his uncle, the Admiral, and all that had happened since they had been separated.

Jack let out a low whistle while they walked up *Twenty-Three*'s gangplank.

"That's quite the tale, mate. And is this your ship?"

"Aye," Wilam dug his fingernails into his palm, forming little crescent wounds into his flesh. It bothered him that this was 'his' ship. It was stolen from some other captain. The captain who was swinging high up in the gallows above the harbor.

"She's a beauty," Jack commented, running his blackened fingers over the dark balustrade. Wilam led Jack down the hold and into the bottom decks, coming to a small room. In the room were a washbasin, a bed, a thick quilt, a small mirror, and a lantern. Jack went inside, nodding to Wilam.

"It's very nice," he said softly. "Thank you,"

"Hopefully, I'll be back soon with Kathryn's father. You can rest here and get cleaned up." Wilam said.

Wilam walked out from below decks and paused by the door to his captain's room. It was quiet. He didn't hear a sound. He considered knocking and asking how the girl was doing but thought better of it, telling himself that Kathryn would be furious if she couldn't come with him. He hesitated a moment longer then left down the gangplank once again.

Chapter Thirty-Three

Kathryn kicked at the wooden oak door after Wilam had locked her in there. He had no right to do this! She could stay hidden from the Admiral without Wilam's help. She could continue to stay with Anna, Charles, Claire, and Meg.

Kathryn groaned. Anna and Meg would not know where she was. She hated herself for letting them go away so quickly.

The girl slumped down against the door and drew her knees up to her chest. Her heart hammered against her ribs.

Why would Wilam lock her in here? Because he feared that much about her safety? Or maybe he wanted to protect her because he loved her…

Quickly, Kathryn dismissed the thought. Rafe had told her that he loved her, and he had been despicable and cruel to her. If that was love, Kathryn wanted none of it. How was Wilam different than Rafe if he locked her up like a prisoner? What was he planning to do with her after he got back?

"I hate him," Kathryn whispered fiercely. And she almost believed herself. Almost.

An hour passed, and Kathryn had barely moved from her place by the door. She just sat, staring at nothing while her thoughts whirled ceaselessly in her head. She didn't even bother looking around her for there was literally nothing to see in the spacious captain's quarters. She thought about what Charles had told her this morning about Jesus. Could Jesus really bring her hope?

Suddenly she sat up, a new thought dawning on her. Hate led to darkness. Love led to light. It all made sense to her now. Love was light. Hate was darkness. Love was good. Hate was bad. As simple was that. If Jesus love was light, then Jesus' light was love. And love conquered darkness.

Kathryn knew she couldn't hate Wilam.

She wanted light.

She wanted real love.

"Jesus," she stuttered hesitantly. "Jesus, I'm scared. I don't want to live in the darkness anymore. I want to have peace and love that I can feel, like what Charles told me about. Please help me. I want to believe you are real and that you will give me real love, but I'm not sure…"

The presence that she had felt those many days ago when she sat in the crow's nest looking at the stars, the comforting, dwelling presence, surrounded her. In an instant, she knew that her prayer had not gone unheard. Someone had listened. Jesus had listened, and He was assuring her that He was there.

Instantly, she felt warm and comforted. Peace settled over her.

Jesus' love was real. She was now sure of it.

"Thank you," she prayed, smiling. "Yes, thank you. I believe now."

Finally, after a long while, Kathryn slowly stood up. She wandered aimlessly around her prison. A desk sat in the corner and a dusty, extinguished lantern hung over it. The room was not cluttered. It had hardly been used at all, for there was literally nothing in it. The window still stood ajar from when Wilam had opened it, and far below it rolled the swells of the tide. In the other corner, an open doorway led to a small room with a bed and nightstand. A quilt and a sheet was the only decoration on the bed, or in the entire bedroom for that matter. She opened the desk drawers, finding nothing but spider webs. Everything had been cleared out, but it wasn't that long ago. Kathryn still saw places in the worn wooden desk where the dust was not settled evenly, like the place where a stack of papers would have been. The inkwell still had a bit of dry ink in it, also.

Kathryn ran her finger across the desk and looked at the dust collected on her finger. It made a streak across the wood. She sighed and began to scribble in the dust. She made odd, swirly pictures with her finger and then wrote her name. She wrote her father's name and then Wilam's. Suddenly, she grew frustrated that she was still thinking about Wilam. She vigorously scrubbed out the boy's name with her palm that at once turned grey with the dust. She slammed down her hand, satisfied by her destruction of the name she so detested at that moment, and was surprised when the desk thumped hollow under her palm. There was no drawer directly under the middle where she had struck.

"Strange," she said quietly. She thumped again, and heard the echoing sound once more. There was definitely a large hollow in the desk that wasn't a regular drawer.

Curious, Kathryn searched for anything that would reveal the hidden hollow. She pulled on the wooden surface from the edge until she felt the wood give. She pried it open, grunting from the labor of the rusty hidden hinges.

A yellowed envelope rested in a small, shallow box built into the frame of the furniture. Kathryn reached inside and pulled it out, smudging grimy fingerprints on the document. The desk slammed shut as Kathryn let it go, dust exploding in the room.

She wiped her hands on the front of her brown apron, coughing and fanning the dirt out of her emerald green eyes. She ran to the window and breathed the sea air. She peered through the yellowed paper as she held the envelope to the light. Turning it over, Kathryn slipped her finger under the edge of the flap and tore it open.

Chapter Thirty-Four

As Wilam was walking about the city, he neared the town square; a giant courtyard that was generally used as a market. Now, however, Wilam grew curious. Most of the crowd was relatively quiet.

Wilam pushed his way through the mass, but nearly everyone simply parted for him due to his coat that indicated his rank. Several people looked at him in fear.

A whip snapped. A moan.

Wilam finally got to the front of the crowd, horrified to see a clearing with a whipping post set up in the middle.

Stripped to the waist with his hands bound to the wooden post above him, Rafe Norrington flinched and cried out again as the whip cracked over his welted back once more. He bit his lip, hard, and swallowed, arching his back in an attempt to dull the fiery lash.

Wilam could only stare, his hands trembling. The boy was younger than him! Even though Wilam had attacked him only a few nights before, he felt pity towards him.

The Admiral watched silently, with not so much as a blink, at the spectacle that he, no doubt, had ordered.

Crack. Crack. Crack. Crack.

Blood trickled down the teenager's back. He had stopped crying out, as he was too weak to do anything but accept his penalty.

At twenty lashes, the whipping stopped. The Admiral stepped over to Rafe. He wrapped his hand in the boy's blonde hair and jerked his head up.

Rafe whimpered.

"Let this be a lesson to you," the Admiral spat in the boy's face. "I am captain."

"You are captain," came Rafe's rasping whisper.

"You will do as I command. Nothing more. Nothing less. If you let the girl get away, then find her. If you report the prisoners, then report them immediately. Understand?"

"Aye, sir."

"You are a failure."

The Admiral let the boy's head drop, then turned the opposite way. He left down a street followed by three guards in black and silver. The crowd thinned, but two lone figures hurried over to the bloodied teenager.

Wilam walked silently over to the figures, surprised to see that they were women. A mother and her daughter. They didn't notice him.

"Rafe," Wilam heard the older woman whisper. Rafe raised his head, looking at them deliriously.

"Why are you here?" he rasped. "I said…"

"Hush. I know what you said. I don't care. Do you want me to leave you to die here?"

"Don't let Meg look at me."

"You remembered my name," the daughter said, shocked.

"Course. Don't look at me."

"If you let us bring you home," Meg said.

"It's not my home anymore,"

"Rafe, please!"

"Just cut the ropes down." Rafe coughed.

"We're forbidden to have weapons. I'll untie it." said Anna, uncertainly. A pause.

Rafe suddenly felt the ropes being sawed. He stumbled weakly as the ropes gave, landing against a strong body.

"Who is this?" Rafe asked in a dull, lifeless voice. Strong, but gentle hands hefted the boy up, careful not to touch the open wounds on his back.

"Wilam Drake," Wilam said. "Where do you want me to take him, ladies?"

Chapter Thirty-Five

Kathryn sank to the ground, reading the worn paper. She tossed the empty envelope aside.

Theodore Sterne,

I am depicting this letter to you through my colleague, Erich; as my hands are bandaged and wounded. I am not as wounded as the rest of my crew, however, and that is good. The pirate attacked my ship, and we could not hold him off. Several of the men suffered greatly at the hand of the black villain. He is dark and wretched, thoroughly undefeatable. I discovered this as I was honored to spar with him by the use of our rapiers. I was surprised to discover that he wears a suit of chain mail under his coat that covers him shoulders down. Where he obtained it, I do not know. Every stab rendered useless, my friend, though I was fighting my best. I know how badly you wish to defeat him, and I can only give you two pieces of advice: Destroy the ship you are in, and every other one you can. This way he has no army. The other proposal I suggest is to hang him. Though heaven knows how you will be able to do that. A man like that doesn't just die. I have tried, my friend, but as I said earlier, my hands are rendered useless and broken. Approach him as a last resort. He will not hesitate to kill you.

Sincerely, Damian Oradel

Chapter Thirty-Six

Wilam closed the door behind him and faced Anna and Meg. Claire hid behind her mother's skirts, shyly peeking out at the handsome young man.

"He's sleeping now. I believe he'll be all right. It was only twenty lashes, and he's strong." Wilam said.

"Thank you so much," Anna said. She frowned suddenly. "Where is Kathryn?"

"Kathryn?"

"Yes, I left her with you when we were called to help with the ship."

"She…she…she is on the ship…"

"Why?"

"I have to protect her."

"From who?"

"The Admiral. She escaped from Ra…her guard before he could put her with her father in the galleys."

"I see," Anna nodded, hesitantly.

"How do you know Rafe? You seem very concerned for his worthless hide," Wilam couldn't hide the bitterness in his voice. Anna looked flustered, and Meg bit her lip, glancing to her mother.

"He's a…a friend." Anna stuttered.

"He's my older brother," Claire said from behind her mother, hiding once again. Meg gasped.

"Hush, Claire." Anna's shoulders slumped, and she turned to Wilam. "Well, you know now,"

"If he should know, than he also should realize that Raeford is a half brother. *I* am not fully related to him, and neither is Claire." Meg crossed her arms, glaring at Wilam. He felt uncomfortable.

"Margaret!" Anna's face was red with embarrassment and anger.

"It's true, Mama. You can't act as if it isn't!" Meg cried, tears threatening to spill down her flushed cheeks. "He shouldn't even be here. He's been nothing but trouble and tension in this family! He never came back, Mama!"

Meg burst into tears and ran from the room.

"Perhaps I bid you good day," Wilam said, awkwardly. Anna snapped her gaze back to the young captain, a thousand emotions flashing through her eyes.

"Yes, perhaps you should," she softly replied. "But give these to Kathryn. She left them here."

She handed the boy a bundle of clothes and he tucked them under his arm.

"And Wilam?" he turned back once again to face the woman. "Take good care of Kathryn. Hear?"

He nodded solemnly, and then turned and left the small house.

He turned his scattered thoughts towards focusing on finding Kathryn's father as he had promised.

Chapter Thirty-Seven

Footsteps sounded outside the wooden door. Kathryn thrust the paper into her bodice, standing quickly. A voice was humming a tune cheerfully. It didn't sound like Wilam.

"Jack?" Kathryn pressed her ear to the grain of the door. "Jack, is that you?"

"Miss Thatcher?" the voice was muffled, but was definitely Jack. The handle rattled. "What are you doing in there?"

"He locked me in here,"

"Who?"

"Wilam did. He said it was to keep me safe, but, oh Jack!"

"What is it?"

"I found something in the desk."

"Aye?"

"Aye, yes. Here, can you read? I'll slide it under the door."

"Aye, I can read."

Kathryn slipped the parchment out of her dress and under the door. She felt the hands grasp it and then withdraw. It was silent for a few, unbearable moments.

"What do you think?" she finally asked.

"Who the hell is Damian Oradell?"

"Who cares? What do you think about the whole letter?"

"Interesting and useful."

"Really?"

"No." he teased.

"Jack!"

She heard his laughter. How foreign that sound was to her ears these days!

"Should we show it to Will?" Jack asked. Kathryn thought for a few moments.

"I…I suppose you can,"

"He'll be back with your father, I believe," Jack said.

"I hope so."

Chapter Thirty-Eight

The Admiral was nowhere to be found, no doubt he was also preparing for the attack. Wilam searched the best he could for Thomas Thatcher, but no such luck. The sun was low in the sky…only one more day until the fleet was launched.

Wilam decided to return to the ship, hoping that George had loaded it properly. Wilam was already doing a dreadful job at being a captain. He looked up at the rotting body hanging high above the harbor and shuddered.

He wanted to rebel against the Admiral, but the man would let no one stop him from fulfilling his reverie.

Wilam climbed up the gangplank to the deck, nodded to the night watchmen, and went to the captain's quarters.

"Will," Jack called from his room. Wilam paused, his hand on the key to unlock the captain's door to see Kathryn. He turned to his friend.

"Aye?"

"Read this," Jack came out and thrust a piece of paper in front of Wilam's face. Wilam pushed it away, embarrassed.

"Jack, you know I can't read," Wilam said. "Tell me what it says later, all right? I need to…see to some business,"

Jack nodded, then left. Wilam clicked the door open, walking inside. He shut the door behind him. The room was dark, so Wilam lit the three lanterns in the room.

"Kathryn?" he said, quietly. He set her little bundle of clothes on the desk and peered around. He found her after a moment, leaning against a darkened corner of the wall, curled up and asleep. He looked at her. Gentle and serene, her face was relieved of the tension that Wilam thought was always present there. Her breathing was even and undisturbed. Wilam thought her beautiful.

He touched her shoulder, and she jerked awake, obviously frightened.

“What…who…what…?” she stuttered, her eyes adjusting to the lantern’s flickering light.

“It’s only me, Kathryn,” he said. She stood up hastily, rubbing her eyes and yawning. Her hair was tousled around her shoulders.

“Oh…Wilam,” she replied bleakly. “Did you get my papa?”

“Nay…I will tomorrow. It was too late,” he said. Her shoulders slumped. “But, I brought your dresses from your friend Anna,”

He pointed to the bundle on the desk. She smiled slightly.

“Thank you,” Kathryn stretched and went to the window, looking out at the stars.

“I have a small room for you to stay in, down the hall,” Wilam said. Kathryn didn’t look at him.

“I'm not tired anymore. And I would rather stay with Anna and Meg,” she said.

“I just saw them…they aren’t…available tonight,” Wilam thought of Rafe, whipped and bloody. He reached into his pocket, fingering the journal and necklace. *No, not here. Not now.* He thought.

"Do you want to walk down to the harbor with me?" he asked, nervously.

Kathryn bit her lip, not looking at him. She felt no anger towards him anymore. The cold blade of the knife pressed against her leg where she had strapped it after Rafe had given it to her. She felt safe and secure with it. But something held her back and told her she wouldn't need it. She could trust Wilam.

"Yes," she said to Wilam's surprise. "I would love to."

Chapter Thirty-Nine

The air was cool against Kathryn's face as she and Wilam walked in a comfortable silence side by side. The ocean crashed against the rocks by the harbor and the moon illuminated the two lone shadows that walked along the sea-worn stones.

"I have something of yours," Wilam broke the silence. Both young people stopped, and Kathryn faced Wilam.

"You do?"

Her question was answered when Wilam took her hand and placed her journal into her palm.

"My journal!" she cried. Wilam also held out the simple gold chain and leaf, the moonlight glinting off of it. Kathryn stared at it, her green eyes suddenly flooded with tears. She wiped them away before they could fall.

Her fingers brushed Wilam’s as she picked the necklace up out of his hand. She was speechless while she stared at it.

“I thought this was lost forever,” she whispered, her voice barely audible. “It was my mother’s.”

“It was?”

“Yes,” Kathryn didn’t say anything after that. She held it out to Wilam, and he took it. She turned around, sweeping her hair to one side. He looped the chain around her neck and fastened the gold clasp. She turned back to Wilam; her hand touched his a moment before she pulled it back. She thumbed through her notebook and glanced at the pages.

“I did look through it,” Wilam said, feeling as if he should tell her. She looked up at him sharply.

“You read my journal?”

“No, I can't read, remember?”

“Oh, yes. That’s right,” she turned back to her journal. She wasn’t angry.

“I saw the pictures you drew.”

“Oh…” she blushed. “So you saw that I sketched you.”

"Aye," he grinned, his white teeth flashing in the silvery moonlight. She smiled back and then touched the little golden leaf at her throat.

"Thank you, Wilam," she said, "For giving this to me."

He embraced her, and then pulled her away slightly. His eyes went over her face, taking in every one of her features till they rested on her eyes once more. She held her breath suddenly as he bent down towards her lips. She shied away. Instead, she embraced him, and he pulled her closely to his chest.

"You are very brave, Miss Kathryn Thatcher," he whispered. She looked up at him.

"My papa gave me a middle name," she said. Wilam looked at her peculiarly. It was a strange change of subject, he thought.

"Aye?"

"Bravery." She rested her head on his broad shoulder, and he laid his chin atop her dark head. "Kathryn Bravery Thatcher."

"It's a beautiful name," he said, "It suits you."

Both of them gazed into the other's eyes after a moment. They leaned close together, their lips nearly touching. A gentle, salty breeze blew over the silent waters, and Wilam's eye caught a movement, a shadow, on the pier. The dreamlike moment was shattered when Wilam stiffened.

"What is it?" Kathryn asked. He lightly gripped her hand.

"Come, we have to get back to the ship. Now."

The shadow stood, menacingly watching the two as they quickly and silently jumped hand in hand down the rocks on the beach. The dark cloak hid his figure, but a sliver of moonlight shone off of his hooded face as he turned slowly to walk down the pier. The Admiral smiled forebodingly until the figures disappeared down the harbor and onto a ship.

Wilam and Kathryn went down to the lower decks of *Twenty-Three* anxiously.

"Who was it?" Kathryn asked breathlessly.

"I…couldn't be sure, but I assumed it was either my uncle or George. It could have been anybody. I don't know."

"Oh."

Wilam handed her the little bundle of clothes off of his desk and she took them, grateful to find a cloak with the garments. He picked up a lantern and lit it.

"Here. I'll show you to your room, and you can get some sleep tonight."

"You have a lot of rooms here," she commented, following him down the darkened hallways. His lantern flickered on the wooden walls as they approached the door.

"Aye," Wilam opened the door for Kathryn as she stepped inside. "I don't have much crew on this ship."

"Are you loyal to the Admiral, Wilam?" she asked timidly.

"Nay," Wilam replied. "I feel no obligation to obey him at all, and nor do I intend to."

"All right. Good night."

"Good night, Kathryn."

He smiled, hung the lantern in her room, and shut the door, being sure not to lock it. He stopped by Jack's room to instruct him to be on guard for Kathryn's safety, and then left the ship. He dreaded leaving her and his ship, but he had to talk to his uncle.

Chapter Forty

It was well past midnight when Wilam came to the Admiral's residence, the slate grey granite house. He let himself inside and shut the door behind him. As he was walking down the marble halls, he was startled to see the Admiral standing in the entrance to the dining room, as if waiting for him.

"Wilam," the Admiral tersely greeted his nephew.

"Uncle,"

"Come have coffee with me in the dining room," the Admiral invited. Wilam followed the man to the dining room where two steaming cups of strong coffee were set out for them. Wilam and his uncle took a seat and sat across from one another. Wilam took a cup and wrapped his fingers around it, absorbing the warmth of the drink.

"I need your help, Wilam," the Admiral began.

"With what?" Wilam asked. He stared skeptically at his uncle as he sipped his drink. The man didn't reply for a long while. When he finally looked up at Wilam, his eyes were wild.

"It's almost time, my boy, for the fleet to launch," he said, "I've wanted this for years. Years! I finally have all my ships, all my captains. My power is unstoppable. I can wave my hand and have a man killed. Yes, Wilam, I am powerful." he leaned back in his chair.

"Why do you need my help?"

"See, I have this young captain. He is talented, good looking, and a natural captain. I admire him. He has only one problem…"

"What's that?" Wilam began to suspect whom the Admiral was speaking of.

"He isn't terribly *focused*…He is given all that a young man his age could possibly want and more. Power, authority, leadership. His one distraction is…restricting to my captain. He cannot seem to think of anything else."

"Who are you talking about?" Wilam asked, already knowing the answer.

"You," the Admiral said, "and that girl."

Wilam grew silent. His uncle was devious. He was trying to trap his young nephew.

"What do you want?" Wilam asked slowly.

"Something simple. It's not too hard…"

"What?"

"Your loyalty." The Admiral turned his stony gaze to Wilam.

"My loyalty?"

"Aye. That is all it takes. You see, Wilam," the Admiral stood up and began pacing the room. "I am not confident that I have your absolute allegiance. I must be sure of your faithfulness to me for three reasons. One, you are my nephew...my only living relative, which brings us to reason two…I need you as my heir to my fleet if and when I die. That is, only if I can be sure you swear to your duty to follow in my footsteps."

"Reason three?" Wilam asked. He was becoming tired of asking all the questions. The Admiral faced his nephew.

"The third reason is this: If you refuse this offer, there will be dire consequences. Not only for you, but also those you love... I see something in you, Wilam, and

I don't want to eradicate such a promising young man. But, the issue is, I don't entirely trust you."

"How could you? I don't trust you, either."

"It doesn't have to be this way, Wilam."

"So you are forcing me to pledge my allegiance to you."

"Not exactly…just affirming the penalty for refusing." The Admiral returned to his seat across from Wilam. The boy was silent, pondering his uncle's words that hung wraithlike in the air.

"What do I have to do?" Wilam finally said. The man smiled coldly and leaned back in his chair.

"To make the oath of allegiance, you must comply with a single command I will give to you," he paused.

"What is it?" Wilam crossed his arms, awaiting the request impatiently.

"Kill the girl." The Admiral smiled as Wilam exploded, jumping up and planting his palms on the table. The coffee cup tipped and sloshed over the woodwork. Neither noticed.

"It was you!" he yelled, "It was you who I saw on the pier! You saw us together on the beach! You intended this, didn't you? Didn't you?"

"Aye," the Admiral chuckled and coolly leaned back again, eyeing his nephew. He enjoyed watching the anger blast out of the boy. He was untamed. He was fierce.

"The prisoners on the ship that you will give to me, Kathryn's father, and everyone else are just a pawn on your little chessboard of life."

"Aye again," the man folded his hands on the table. "Once we get out on the sea, if you still have not killed the girl, I sink your ship and everyone on it. Boom, boom, boom! Fire and hell everywhere. And it will be your entire fault. Of course, that is assuming you refuse to carry out my little request. It shouldn't be too difficult, should it?"

Wilam seethed, digging his fingernails into the table. He wanted to kill the man.

"You would destroy one of your own ships…to destroy me?" he said through clenched teeth. His hand drifted to the hilt of his cutlass.

"If you anger me by disobeying, I will make you pay. I won't even care if it is my own ship."

"Then you will destroy your chance to change me. You know you want me to be like you. I will never be like you!" Wilam shouted.

"Yes you will…I need you. If I can't have you…hell, I will kill you. So kill the girl. Get rid of her. You will then have my trust and I will spare your life. I will promote you to the highest ranks. You will be head captain. You will have this island when I die. The army will be yours…everything will be yours."

"So I save my own life and all the lives of my crew by killing Kathryn?" Wilam snarled. "I won't do it. I won't kill her. You are a crazy old man and don't know what you are talking about."

"Indeed, I am crazy. You will kill her. Or else I will. I will murder her before your eyes and then I will do the same to you. She will be in so much pain…" the Admiral's face contorted with bloodlust. "Or, you could kill her quickly and save your life and the lives of your crew."

"You son of the devil…" Wilam fumed.

"Why don't you go rest," the Admiral said to his nephew calmly. "You look a bit piqued."

Wilam pushed back rapidly, throwing his chair back from the table, and stormed out of the room. The door forcefully slammed behind him. The Admiral sighed slowly and sipped his coffee. Inside, he was excited and jovial, so much that he couldn't even think of going to sleep.

He decided to stay up. Tomorrow, he decided he would place many people on Wilam's ship to make the pressure all the more apprehensive for Wilam. Of course, the people would be mere peasants...no loss to the Admiral. Wilam would certainly care. He was too sentimental and soft for a Drake. It made the Admiral sick.

He had a reason for making Wilam kill the girl. It would make him stronger and calloused. He would become cold and heartless like his uncle and turn from all things that would make him happy. Wilam would be ruthless and powerful, and no one could stop him. He would live up to his name as a Drake. He would bring honor and power to the Admiral's reputation.

That is...if Wilam decided he would kill the girl and get over with it.

He wanted Wilam to be like him. He wanted Wilam to *be* him. Even now, as the Admiral sat quietly and serenely, he knew it was probably too late. Wilam was almost a man…a real man. He would make his own choices. But, even while a young child working on his ship so many years ago, Wilam had always wanted to be a captain. The Admiral remembered the light in his young nephew's eyes when the boy saw the plundered gold and riches.

The thing was, Wilam was a natural seaman. He was literally born at sea when his mother gave birth on the ship to New Harbour seventeen years before. The Admiral was actually impressed with his long-lost nephew, except for his love for the useless girl who changed him; who had made him soft. She must be done away with. Wilam was distracted and not focused on his job. The Admiral had watched the boy as he neglected his duties to be with the girl on the beach. He needed a man like Wilam. Soon. And without the worthless complication of teenage love. Wilam had to kill Kathryn.

"He must, Drake. There is no other way…" the Admiral rocked back and forth, gazing wildly out the window with glassy eyes. "But I cannot know if I can trust the boy. Yes, you can...but you must make him ruthless. You must change him! I will...I can...Wilam! Sickening. The girl. Why is it always a girl? A man goes from cold-blooded to kindhearted in a matter of seconds when there is a girl..."

The Admiral stopped for a long while. He didn't even blink. His eyes flashed as he argued within himself.

"Blood...I must have blood. Blood is domination. Blood is power."

He stood, pacing the hall angrily. His mind was clouded with his insanity. He ran his fingers through his tousled hair and then reached for his cutlass. With a cry of feral enraged ferocity, he swung the blade above his head. It impaled the wall. He wrenched it out and swung again. And again. And again. The wall was slashed with shredded, gaping openings, like wounds on a rotting corpse. The Admiral collapsed in his chair, panting and dripping with sweat.

His nephew must not intervene with his plan to conquer the harbor the Admiral so coveted.

Chapter Forty-One

The next morning proved gloomy and overcast, matching Wilam's mood. He clutched the wheel in his hand, his eyes red-rimmed and nervous. Standing on the deck of the ship *Twenty-Three*, Kathryn and Jack looked out at the island a few hundred yards away from them. The ship was circling the island on a trial run, with Wilam Eugene Drake as the captain. Several other ships navigated in front of and behind *Twenty-Three*, completing their test runs also.

Clouds blotted the sky, and a cool, gusty breeze propelled the ships forward, nearly in unison.

Wilam gave orders to the men and made sure that all of the sails, mast yards, rudder, and everything else was in its proper position. George was practically taking over the ship, however, giving most of the orders and such. He never talked to Wilam, nor gave him a second glance. Whenever he had to look at the boy, his face was full of disgust and resentment. He was an experienced seaman, Wilam noticed. Wilam decided long ago to just let the man have his space.

With the trial run around the island done, Wilam turned the ship to the docks. As the gusts of wind thrust the ship forward, Wilam detected a scent of rain in the atmosphere. The sky contained little clouds, but Wilam could tell that a storm was silently brewing in the atmosphere.

His thoughts drifted to the strange letter Kathryn had found in his desk. He and Jack had had a meeting early in the morning over the letter, and Wilam had found it intriguing. A trifling bit of research by Jack confirmed that the author of the letter, Damian Oradell, was no more than a middle-aged seaman who was captured by the Admiral two years before. He had perished only a few months before the hanging of Sterne. Wilam thought the letter was interesting. How long had it been sitting in Sterne's desk before Kathryn found it? Apparently, the letter was the reason Sterne had been hanged. It instructed him to destroy the ships instead of face the man himself.

And what about the part that said the Admiral was guarded and armored with chain mail? Wilam chuckled slightly. If the fact was true, it hinted that the Admiral was paranoid, if not fearful, of being killed or hurt. So he wasn't as tough and sure as he made himself out to be.

Wilam, who was steering the large sloop, glanced at Kathryn and Jack at the bow of the ship, talking quietly together. He hadn't told her or Jack about what the Admiral had commanded him, concerning the death of Kathryn. Wilam knew he couldn't kill anyone, let alone the girl he loved. Did he love her? Wilam couldn't keep his eyes off of her. He had almost kissed her last night. Why hadn't he? He cursed his sneaking and spying uncle. Did Kathryn feel affection for him as much as he thought he did her? Was she only about to kiss him because he had given her something treasured and dear to her? Oh, how that night went from wonderful to awful in such a short time, he didn't know. After his talk with the Admiral, Wilam had stumbled onto his ship slightly drunk. He had been so upset that he had gone to a tavern to drink his fear away. It hadn't helped a bit, but rather had given him a splitting headache in the morning when he woke. Even if Kathryn didn't love him, he still wanted to keep his promise to her that she would see her father. Love was such a complicated subject. He barely even knew what it meant. The Admiral had threatened to destroy all the people on his ship if he didn't kill the girl, and that included her father as well. When the Admiral came around distributing the prisoners on the ships, Wilam hoped he could still get Kathryn's father. He hoped that he would be able to fulfill that promise to her when the Admiral distributed the prisoners. Wilam had promised Kathryn that she would be able to see her father that day. He didn't intend to break it…even if she didn't love him. What could he do? He could leave her on the island and say that he had killed her. Yes. That was it. Then he could come back for her after he destroyed the Admiral. Yes. He would leave her and her father on the island.

Shaking his head, Wilam cleared his thoughts and focused on turning the big ship's wheel. Carefully, the ship was docked, and this time, it was in it's numerical order, to the right of *Twenty-Two* and to the left of *Twenty-Four*.

As the sloop was being secured on the harbor, Wilam had the gangplank lowered to the wooden pier.

Through the rush of people coming to and from the ships' dock, Wilam soon lost sight of Kathryn and Jack as they melted into the crowd. He wanted to talk to her; he hadn't conversed with her the entire day. He only wanted to be by her, to walk with her, to see her brilliant green eyes one more time. He may never come back on the island for her. He may be lost at sea. He may be destroyed along with his ship.

It is better this way, Wilam thought, *Right now, I need to get her father...and the other prisoners. I can't break that promise to her. Besides, it's clear that she hates me.*

And he strutted down the gangplank on his mission.

Chapter Forty-Two

Friday,

The time is now for the Admiral's big move. He will attempt to destroy the city on the morrow, and there is nothing anyone can do about it. Jack told Wilam about the letter, and I do not know what he thinks of it. I don't even know whose side he is really on. The main man we are trying to stop is his uncle! Last night was strange. Wilam seems to come up in every thought I think about today. I don't even know my feelings for him. He is dangerous, very dangerous. But, I can't help but feel an attraction between us. He promises to bring my father onto the ship today, and although I am very excited, something was not right as we were doing the trial sailing around the island. Wilam is not acting his normal self. I think something is wrong, and I don't think that it is stress. I shall bring up to date my notebook with all that has happened in the past week since I lost it, whenever I have spare time. ~Kathryn

Kathryn looked up from her corner of the deck. She did not wish to disembark from the ship, as there was a large crowd of peasants and sailors who made it nearly impossible to maneuver around without getting crushed.

“Jack,” Kathryn called up to her friend. Jack was still on the ship, mending the black sails like he used to do on the *Farrow.* He looked down at her from the foremast yard, pulled on a rope and tied it tight in an intricate sailor’s knot. “Have you heard from Captain Halkins lately?”

“Nay, Miss Kathryn. All I know is that he’s back on the *Farrow.* They renamed it Number *Forty.* I really haven't seen him since we were brought to the island. The man to ask is Will. He may know more than I do.”

“Alright,” Kathryn said and thanked him. She glanced around the busy deck, not locating Wilam. She didn’t expect to see him, and she didn’t want to go out and find him. She would wait until he came back onto his ship.

As she leaned against the balustrade and looked over the bustling harbor, her attention was drawn to a crowd of people. It was a mob, a mass of people coming down the harbor and pier. Ordinary peasants moved out of the way, confused at what was going on.

The sound of a whip snapped through the air, and Kathryn squinted against the sun. A mass of slaves and prisoners were being herded onto the ships. Some ships were loaded with several, some with only one or two. They approached *Twenty-Three*, and George came on board, followed by Wilam and eleven prisoners. The deck was so full of people that Kathryn couldn't see who the prisoners were.

After George announced something and unshackled the captives, he left, and they were herded into the lower decks. Kathryn didn't see her father as the captives went past her. Disappointment knifed through her.

Pushing her way towards where Wilam stood, she appeared behind him and tugged on the elbow of his grand coat. He turned and faced her. His eyes showed a hint of sadness and seemed…burdened.

"Aye, Kathryn?" he said.

"Did you get my papa?" she asked softly. He nodded and her heart leaped. "Where is he?"

Wilam took her hand. "He's below decks with the others. You probably didn't recognize him because he had a cloak covering him. He's not…he isn't doing well, Kathryn. I had to barter for him, but I got him."

"Can I go see him, Wilam?"

"Aye. Do you want me to take you down there?"

"Yes," she said. Wilam released his slight grip on her hand, almost reluctantly, and led the way down below the deck.

They came to the lower deck, and Kathryn saw a hammock swinging gently from the rafters. Eagerly, the girl rushed over to it. A man lay there.

"Papa, it's me." She whispered. The pale, wasted man turned his gaunt face to her, breathing hard, as if he had just ran. She bit back the repulsion that arose in her throat. Her father looked much worse than when she had seen him so many days ago in the Admiral's courtyard. His hair was thin and nearly white. He looked double his forty-four years, with dry skin and watery, bloodshot eyes.

"Tip," he whispered, his voice barely audible. He reached out a bony hand and Kathryn grasped it in her own, shaking with dismay at how cold and lifeless his hand felt. He closed his eyes and then opened them again, taking a deep breath to slow his panting. He looked at his daughter.

"What did they do to you, Papa?" Kathryn asked, desperately wanting to know how to help her father.

"Kathryn," Wilam said softly from behind her. She had forgotten that he was still in the room. She looked at her friend with tears in her eyes. "Don't make him remember right now. I am having food and water brought to him. He's been starved and beaten and…you get it." Wilam motioned to the sick man, and Kathryn looked at her father once more.

"Kathryn…" he said through cracked lips. "Why are you here? Where did you come from? Are you all right?"

"I'm fine, Papa. I came with John Halkins. Surely you remember seeing me a few days ago…?" Kathryn trailed off. He wouldn't remember anything. He was too delirious.

A crewmember came to the door, and Wilam took the tray of food that he had brought.

"Here, Kathryn, see if you can get him to eat anything." Wilam held the food out to the girl. She took it without a word. Wilam watched her spoon the soup into her Papa's mouth for a few moments.

"You should stay on the island," Wilam finally said. Kathryn looked at him harshly.

"Why? What about papa?"

"He should stay too. You can care for him on the island. Please, Kathryn. It's for your own safety," he was begging her.

She glanced at him with hurt shining abusively in her eyes. She looked away from him and focused on her papa.

"I can't stay on this evil island, Wilam," she whispered, "Papa's going to die."

"I just want you safe…" he moaned.

"Why are you like this? Why do you so desperately not want me on your ship?"

"I'm afraid you will…you will be hurt. Please, listen to me. I will try to come back for you…I'm just so afraid that something will go wrong,"

"No. I will stay on the ship. I can't be on that island, Wilam." Tears pooled in the corners of her green eyes and she brushed them away before they could fall. She was always in terror on that cursed island. She would die there from constant worry. No, she would stay on that ship. If she died, so be it.

Wilam saw that he could not convince her, so he left alone, returning to the deck and to his duty as captain.

Chapter Forty-Three

"We love you, Rafe. Please don't go," my mother begs me. I pull away from her.

"I am not of this family. I'm different. Nobody wanted me to be born in the first place. You didn't want me to be born." I say. I try to keep from yelling at her.

"God gave you to us," my stepfather says in a calm voice. "We accept you as you are. We all love you. You are of this family."

"Do not speak to me of God! He is not real! If he were, he would not have let me be born. I don't even know my real father. I want to be a part of something real, like the fleet. I will have status and rank. I will be respected. Not loved! I don't want your love."

"Rafe," my mother says. "Please. God accepted all of us when we were rejected by sin. He loved us and welcomed us into His eternal family as our father. We are

doing the same for you. We love you and want you in our family."

"Its not our family. It's your family." I turn to my stepfather. "You are not my father. You never will be. God is not my father. He never will be."

They all have tears in their eyes. Mama takes a step towards me: her hand is outstretched to me.

"Rafe, please listen. We love you. We accept you and love you as you are. I will always love you."

"Stay away from me!" I shout. I back up towards the door: I fumble for the handle. I get it open, turn, and flee down the street. Escape. I can't stay. She doesn't understand. They all don't understand.

Rafe Norrington woke that morning in a cold sweat, gasping for breath. He lay back on the pillow. He was on his bed. He looked around his surroundings. He was in the house. He muttered a curse and shifted his weight. His back screamed whenever he moved, but he gritted his teeth and rolled over, flipping his feet off the side of the bed. He had to get away from the house. It held too many painful memories for him. Too much pressure. Too much difference. He slipped his shirt on, trying to ignore the burning sensation that flamed across his back when the soft fabric touched his raw wounds.

"Rafe," his mother whispered from his doorway. He refused to look at her. He stood in front of the flawed, dull mirror washing his battered face gently and combing his fingers through his long, blonde hair. "Please stay. At least until you are well enough. Your back is already starting to bleed from you moving so fast."

"I can't stay, Mama," he finally said. "I just can't stay. You know that."

"But it's been so long…" Anna bit her lip. "And I miss you."

"Does Charles miss me? Does Meg? Claire doesn't even know me. Does she miss me? No. Mama, I'm not wanted here. I've been all right for five years."

"Until now," Anna said softly. Rafe slapped the wet rag into the washbasin and turned to his mother. He was nearly a head taller than she, yet he still felt intimidated by her. He dared not show it.

"Yes, until now. But Mama, I'm going on one of those ships tomorrow to find a life in New Harbour. Alone." He said. "No one to hate me or know me or my past. Or your past, for that matter."

"Rafe..." Anna teared up, "I don't hate you. I just want to know my own son for more than a few minutes. I haven't watched you grow. I rarely see you. When you are gone, I fear I may never see you again."

"It would be better for you," Rafe assumed. Anna shook her head.

"And what about you? Would it be better for you not to see me?"

"Mama..." Rafe murmured incoherently. He wanted to be done with this conversation. Could she not hear the simple reason that was so true? He would leave. She had two daughters now and a husband who loved her. She had her own, comforting religion. She would be happy. Did she not see that he was nothing but a burden?

"I am sorry, Rafe," she said, leaning on the doorframe. He finally looked at his mother, surprised to see pools of tears at the corners of her blue eyes.

"You shouldn't be. I don't see why you even care anymore," he said, heartlessly. He pushed past Anna, marching into the front entrance of the house and placing his hand on the doorknob. "I'm leaving, Mama."

"Wait..." she approached him and looked up into his blue eyes, so much like her own. His face softened when she reached up her hand and brushed a shock of blonde hair back from his forehead. “Know that I still love you. I will always love you, my son. God bless you,”

She reached up and gently kissed his forehead.

He stopped, hesitating. A moment later, he shut the door behind him. He took a deep breath, threw his shoulders back, and stepped into the world.

Chapter Forty-Four

"This day is a great day," the Admiral was saying to the crowds of people. He stood on the hill, his voice carried down to the multitudes at the harbor by a large horn-like contraption. The people were silent as death, not one daring to make a sound. Among them was the small family of girls, Anna, Meg and Claire. They stood by the ship that Charles captained. Charles stood with the rest of the captains by the Admiral. Wilam was at the right side of his uncle, looking uncomfortable and ill at ease.

"This day, we will fulfill the dream of us all. We will take the city of New Harbour for our own, and no one will be able to stop us. You will all have whatever you want, as part of the Black Sailed fleet, for you will be under my protection and rule. I will be a great leader to all of you and swear to protect you with all of my being."

Wilam cringed at the lies his uncle was spewing out on the ignorant peasants of his incarcerated community.

"I, along with my captains," the Admiral continued his speech, gesturing to the men that stood at either side of him, "will lead you wisely and judiciously as long as you continue to pledge your loyalty to them and to me."

The crowd cheered. Wilam noticed, though, that not everyone agreed. Several had mixed looks of anger, indignity, dishonor, doubt, and fear written on their faces as they remained silent and didn't cheer like their neighbors did. Wilam met the eyes of John Halkins. He wore a mask of indifference and apathy, not a trace of emotion on his chiseled face. Halkins turned away from Wilam's gaze and looked to the Admiral.

The remainder of the speech was lost to Wilam as he looked down at the ships gently bobbing in the waves, all of them flying the red flag with the silhouette of a black ship high on their masts. His hazel brown eyes looked down on his ship deck, *Twenty-Three*, down to the girl at the bow. She was scribbling ferociously in her little notebook. She looked up, and Wilam could have sworn she was looking directly at him. His heart jumped suddenly, and he chided himself for feeling like a young child in love. Forgetting his surroundings, Wilam closed his eyes and became painfully aware of the threat that hung over his head. *Kill the girl...kill the girl...all the people on your ship...fire and hell everywhere...your entire fault...kill the girl...kill...* Wilam tensed his body.

The Admiral was going to destroy his ship and all the people on it if he didn't kill Kathryn. He didn't dare hide her on the island now, for this morning his uncle had demanded that Wilam show him the body of the girl after he had killed her.

The crowd cheering once more brought Wilam back to the present. The captains led the way to their ships and Wilam followed. He was jostled and bumped into before he felt a familiar hand on his shoulder. Halkins spun the boy around.

"What the hell is going on, Will?" Halkins spat, looking around desperately as if someone would see him talking to Wilam.

"What do you mean, Captain?"

"Shut up! Don't refer to me as your captain. I mean, what is going on with you and your insanely mad uncle? Quickly, now. I can't be seen talking to you for long."

"I have to kill Miss Thatcher or else he destroys my ship and everyone on it, and he kills her and I. Her father is on my ship and not doing well, and my uncle is loading women and children on your ship, and several other vessels whose captains he believes will try to destroy his fleet. He does this so that the captains won't want to danger them in a fight." Wilam said all in one breath. Halkins let go of the boy's shoulders and took a step back.

"You gonna kill her?" he asked quietly. He watched Wilam's face for any sign. Betrayal. Coldness. Darkness. Like his uncle.

Halkins was testing Wilam.

"I don't aim to. No, sir. I love her." Wilam said, surprised when Halkins started to laugh. He clapped the boy on the arm.

"You are such a young thing. Now, what's the plan?"

Wilam quickly gave him the information. Halkins nodded.

"Sounds smart. Good luck out there today." The old sea captain said.

"You too," Distantly, Wilam turned away as Halkins melted into the crowd, thinking about what the man had said. Not a moment too soon, Wilam heard a harsh voice in his ear.

"Where's the girl's body, Wilam?" the Admiral furiously thrust his face into his nephew's.

"I still have her. I...I haven't had the time. I'll bury her at sea when we are about to attack."

"I want to see her, Wilam. I want to see you kill her." the Admiral's eyes were bright with bloodlust.

"When do you want me to do it?"

"Pull your ship up to mine about one hour after we depart. Bring her over to my ship. You had better be there, Wilam." Suddenly, the resolution to the destruction of the Admiral came to him.

"Aye, sir," Wilam said. The Admiral shook his head sardonically and smirked at his nephew.

"To the ships!" came a thunderous command. The Admiral raised a horn to his lips and blew a deafening blast.

Kathryn Bravery Thatcher looked up from her notebook, dread creeping into her heart.

Wilam Eugene Drake came to the wheel of his ship, biting his lip restlessly. He tucked a pistol into his sash as he glanced towards Kathryn.

Jack Cadett ran onto the ship out of breath, grinning at Wilam. The plan was ready. He watched the ships get into the attack positions, noticing as several ships shifted around.

John Halkins gave orders on his ship to be reallocated to a different position: parallel to Wilam's vessel. No one noticed that he was out of line.

Rafe Norrington crouched by the cannons of John Halkins's ship near all of the other cannon men, determination on his face.

The Admiral, decked in his finest attire and sporting several weapons, sailed his galleon to the very front of the fleet, a menacing grin dominating his striking features.

New Harbour was doomed.

Chapter Forty-Five

Thirty minutes had passed since the departure of the fleet from the island. Wilam loathed the sounds of war cries and battle ready men coming from the other ships around him. He took a deep breath, and then tasted the air. He sensed rain.

Peering up into the sky, he noticed only a few clouds. That didn't mean anything. The sea was impulsive and unpredictable when it came to storms. As if an answer to his doubts, a gusty wind swept across the deck, whipping Wilam's sun bleached hair around his face. The wind was strong, and kept blowing from apparently every direction.

Wilam cursed through gritted teeth.

"Is something wrong, Wilam?" Kathryn came up to him and stood at his side.

"Do you not smell that?" he said, more sharply than he intended.

"Smell what?" Kathryn looked hurt. Right away, Wilam's tone grew softer.

"The rain, the anger of the sky. There's going to be a storm, Kathryn." He sighed. "How is your father?"

"I think he is better. He has been sleeping for a long time now. The color is returning to his skin, and his breathing seems more natural,"

"Sounds like he is doing good."

"Aye, better anyway," she smiled. Wilam looked away. He didn't want to see her smile. If his crazy plan went wrong, and she died…he refused to think about it.

"Wilam, are you all right?"

"Nay," he clenched his jaw. She touched his arm ever so slightly.

"Please, tell me what's bothering you," she begged. Her fingertips felt like they were burning him. He tore his arm away and leaned upon the balustrade, breathless and angry with himself. He was aware of the pistol at his side. As he leaned against the railing, he grew unexpectedly grateful for the storm. It would provide an astonishing advantage to his scheme.

Kathryn stared at him and didn't make another move towards him. She was puzzled at his behavior. She looked up to see their ship approaching the Admiral's vessel. Wilam ran his fingers through his hair and looked determinedly up at the galleon. His hazel brown eyes stung from the wind.

The storm picked up, thrashing around harder and harder as the sky grew dark with clouds, clouds that lit up brilliantly with lightning. Thunder rumbled.

Kathryn looked up suddenly as Wilam took hold of her and pulled her close to himself, his eyes flashing with torn emotions. His lips brushed against her ear as he whispered, "I'm supposed to bring you onto the Admiral's galleon."

"What for?" she asked, alarmed. His arms held her tight. She could feel his fear coursing through his rigid body, and she wrapped her small arms around his chest. He closed his eyes and took deep breaths, resting his chin atop her head. His heart was beating quickly with the fright that he felt. The terror that lashed out from not knowing how his plan would make out, not knowing if Kathryn would be alive when it was all over. Kathryn was thinking the same about Wilam.

"The Admiral wants me to kill you, but I have a different idea." He hugged her fiercely, and then cupped her face in his hands. Another flash of lightning and the roar of thunder vibrated the ship as Kathryn clutched the hands on her face, staring at Wilam. He looked at her sternly. "Trust me, Kathryn. I won't kill you, and nor will I let anyone else. Go below decks and watch over your papa. Don't come above deck for any reason. I have a plan. Trust me…"

"I already do," Kathryn said, squeezing his calloused hand. He smiled, bent towards her, and then kissed her lips softly. A moment later, he pulled away from her and reluctantly thrust her into the arms of Jack, who began to lead her below deck for safety. Kathryn smiled for encouragement when Wilam cast one last glance in her direction before yelling to his men.

"Ready the port cannons!"

They were approaching the black galleon quickly.

From the port side.

The sky opened, and the rain began to fall.

Chapter Forty-Six

John Halkins steered his ship to the starboard side of the black, three-rowed galleon, his cannons at the ready. A crewmate watched Wilam's ship for the next signal. So far, no one noticed *Forty*, the old *Farrow*, getting out of her position. The storm had everyone's attention at that moment, and for that he was indebted. Wilam needed his help, and Halkins would do what he could to assist him.

As Halkins's blue eyes peered through the sheet of rain that was steadily pouring harder and harder, he saw Wilam's ship pull up close to the black galleon. Suddenly, it pulled a bit farther out. A flash of fire and a boom like thunder erupted from *Twenty-Three*'s cannons. The Admiral's black ship cringed, and Wilam took that recover time to retreat further out into the water. The black galleon answered by firing her cannons at Wilam's ship. She was too late, however, and *Twenty-Three* sailed out of the range of the cannons. The iron balls of lead fell harmlessly into the choppy sea.

Angered, the Admiral turned his damaged vessel in pursuit of his nephew. Halkins followed, and proceeded to aim all of his cannons towards the stern of the black galleon. They exploded together, and the sound of splintering wood could be heard even over the roar of the storm. Several balls fell short, and instead crashed into other vessels.

Halkins laughed triumphantly, throwing a proud, dripping fist into the air.

The fleet was soon chaotic as the ships flocked together to take sides. Nearly half went to aid Wilam, and the other half to their Admiral.

His black galleon that the Admiral so admired was damaged, but not paralyzed. Her three rows of oars thrust in and out of the water, moving in harmony with one another. Her cannons went at the ready as the ship sped towards Wilam's vessel. *Twenty-Three* was turning around for another run with the cannons at the galleon, but the Admiral's ship approached too quickly. Churning waters were raging beneath the vessels as the storm intensified drastically. The waves mounted up, throwing billowing swells of water against into the ships.

Before Wilam knew what was happening, the bow of the Admiral's galleon rammed into *Twenty-Three*'s starboard side, running her bow sprit through the ship's flank. The collision splintered the blackened wood of both ships, and crewmembers from both vessels were thrown from their feet.

"Attack!" the Admiral roared, and his pirate crew began to board the wounded *Twenty-Three.*

Halkins pulled his ship over to the battle on the decks of both ships, and his men also jumped into the fight. Soon, all of the ships were at battle, whether in person, or attempting to destroy the ships a few yards away from the wreck. Screams were heard when a ship not far away blew up in a scorching explosion of fire and gunpowder lit together. Dead bodies were cast into the water followed by the few survivors who jumped into the water…choosing to brave the stormy waves than be consumed by the fiery wreck that was sinking below the rolling surface.

Chapter Forty-Seven

Below the deck of *Twenty-Three*, Wilam's ship, Kathryn clutched her father, Thomas. He was stronger, but still weak. He leaned on his daughter for support when the ship pitched. Water began flowing into the hold and pooled around their feet, the level rising steadily. Both of them fell into the salty water when the cannons above them fired and the hold vibrated from the explosion.

"We have to get higher, Papa," Kathryn cried. He only nodded, trusting her judgment. She threw his arm over her shoulder and helped support him as they walked towards the doorway. Kathryn looked around desperately as the water surged around their knees already, making it nearly impossible to hasten their pace.

A crashing force blasted against the ship, throwing splinters and shrapnel around them. Kathryn screamed as a few wooden shards embedded themselves in her back. She had thrown herself in front of her father as a shield from the explosion. Frantic now, she pushed him towards the doorway that could just be seen. Suddenly, Kathryn felt a strong arm pull her instead.

"Who…?" It was her father, a new strength in his eyes and body. He trudged ahead of her, gently guiding her through the debris that surged by in the murky, swirling ocean water surrounding them. Her skirt was weighing her down. It suddenly caught on an unseen snare under the water. She tugged it harshly and the fabric tore free. Thomas slogged towards the doorway until they came within less than a meter away from the door. Abruptly, the ship shuddered, and more water gushed into the rapids. Rubble and wreckage were everywhere, blocking the doorway and causing the hold to fall into nearly complete darkness.

Thomas grunted as he fumbled around in the blackness, tugging at the wood to where he last saw the way out. The water was up to their chests, and Kathryn could no longer keep her feet on the ground. She swam her way to her papa and held onto his shoulders as an anchor.

"How can you see, Papa?" she asked into his ear. He picked up a board and smashed it against the wooden wall.

"I was in a dark hell for five years, rowing an oar. Water was constantly at our feet, peeling off the skin of our feet as we ceaselessly rowed and rowed and rowed. I hated it..." he muttered, then stopped suddenly. "Here's the door. Hold your breath. It's underwater."

Kathryn held her breath. Before she knew what was happening, her father had pushed her below the surface and thrust her through the opening. She came up, sputtering, on the other side and grasped her papa's hands through the doorway. She helped to pull him out.

"There," Thomas pointed in the darkness. Kathryn couldn't see a thing. "We can get to the higher deck if we come to the end of this hallway. The ladder comes to the cannon deck."

Kathryn clutched his arm and they half swam, half walked through the salty ocean water down the ship's hallway.

Chapter Forty-Eight

Wilam scrambled for a foothold as the force of the firing cannons rocked the unsteady ship. Two pirates descended upon him, and he attempted to fire his pistol at them. The powder was wet, so he threw the weapon aside and unsheathed his cutlass. Driving the blade deep into the heart of one, he tore out the sword and thrust it into the gut of the other. As the pirates fell, dead, several more appeared to take their place, all with weapons drawn. Wilam's crew turned on them, and the rain that puddled on the deck was soon mixed with blood. Smoke billowed from the ships from smoking cannons and blazing ships around them.

Out of the corner of his eye, as Wilam was defending his life, he saw several ships approach, Halkins one of them. They pulled up close to the raging battle and Wilam was provided with reinforcements.

Wilam knocked away several blows that would have surely killed him but was rapidly becoming outnumbered. He backed away a step, then slipped and went down hard on the deck. Suddenly, George loomed above him, lightning illuminating his evil face. The man grinned. Raised the sword. Lightning flashed. Wilam braced himself. Halkins jumped in between and parried with the pirate. A few advancing steps and a flick of the wrist threw the weapon out of the George's hand and into Halkins's ready fist. George screamed when Halkins drove the sword into his gut. Halkins then flipped the lifeless man overboard, the hilt of the blade jutting out of George's abdomen. George was gone.

John Halkins turned and helped Wilam to his feet.

"What's the plan?" he asked. Wilam pointed towards the Admiral's galleon that was impaling their ship.

"We defeat the Admiral, get the ships on our side to defeat the Admiral's followers." Wilam paused. "Leave my uncle to me."

"Aye…Captain," Halkins nodded seriously to Wilam and turned to the crew that was still battling the pirates swarming over both vessels to get to his ship.

Wilam clambered through the hoards of men, both good and bad, to get to the black-sailed galleon. In all the nervous tension, Wilam hadn’t noticed his ship was slowly sinking lower and lower into the water. The billows of the sea carried the ships up and down, making it difficult for Wilam to walk in a straight line. He set his jaw determinedly, gripped his cutlass, and pressed on towards the ship that carried his uncle, the Admiral.

Chapter Forty-Nine

Spluttering, Kathryn and her father collapsed on the higher gun deck that contained the cannons. Several crewmen who were firing the cannons helped them out of the hallway from where they had just come. It was surging with water and debris.

"Are you all right?" asked one of the crewmen. Kathryn nodded, coughing, and turned to her father. He crouched on his knees, his head down, trying to regain his strength. He was shaking.

"Papa?" Kathryn knelt next to him, shivering in her wet clothes. He put his arm around her and kissed her forehead.

"I'll be fine, Tip," he said, giving her a slight smile. "I'm only a little weak. Don't worry about me. I've lasted five years in a dark, wet, painful hell already. One more storm won't bring me down."

"Is anyone else down in there?" asked one of the men.

"No, it was just us," Kathryn answered. The crew went on about their figuring out where to fire next.

"It's best if you get out of here," the man said suddenly. "Cannons roar mighty dangerous with fire and gunpowder the like. If we get hit, 'tis worse still. Git yourselves on the main deck, or at least above the guns,"

"Thank you kindly. We will," Thomas stood up slowly, Kathryn at his side.

The ship rocked sharply all of a sudden, and the door to the gun deck flew open, revealing a drenched and dripping young man with a dagger clutched in his hand. He was breathless.

"Everyone, out," he commanded. "Ship's going down. One more wave will finish her. Move, move, move! Get on one of the other ships,"

The men rushed by the young man as he held the door for them against the wind. Kathryn gasped as she passed by him.

Rafe.

He gave her a knowing look as she slipped by with her father to follow the gunmen up to the main deck. Rafe made sure no other people were in the rest of the ship before guiding the way up.

Once on deck, Kathryn was slapped with the torrents of rain stinging her face. In vain, she tried to shield herself from the blinding downpour. Through her squinted eyes, Kathryn could just make out figures scrambling and slipping over the decks, heading towards another ship. Its bowsprit had collided with the ship she stood on now.

Rafe came by her side and she instinctively stepped closer to her father, entwining her arm with his.

"The Admiral's ship is our only hope," Rafe pointed. As if on cue, the ship they stood on shuddered beneath their feet. Kathryn could actually feel the ship collapsing under the weight of the water in the lower decks. A wave loomed up out of the depths. "Go!" shouted Rafe, throwing Thomas's arm over his shoulder as Kathryn took his other arm. They hurried as fast as they could over the slick deck.

Wilam watched in horror from the Admiral's ship as a smaller wave crashed over the depleting vessel next to them. It would be too late for him to get over there to help Kathryn and her father when the next wave came.

Were they still below the deck? He couldn't see them from the angle he was at, for the galleon he was on was positioned higher.

Stumbling over bodies and debris and avoiding the battle that ensued around him, Wilam fought through until he crashed into the railing. There below him were three figures. The rain had let up a bit, and Wilam could make out Kathryn, her father, and Rafe Norrington. Forgetting all of the enmity he had for the boy, Wilam called out to them, waving his hands. Kathryn spotted Wilam and pointed breathlessly up at him.

"It's too high!" she shouted up to him. Wilam looked around desperately. Suddenly, Jack appeared at his side, holding a wet, slimy, ship-worn rope. It was a rope nonetheless. Wilam took it in silent thanks, and then stopped. The hand Jack was holding the rope out to him with had two bloodied stumps where a couple of his fingers used to be. Wilam looked into Jack's blue eyes, his brows were knitted together in concern. Jack shrugged then helped Wilam to tie the rope to the balustrade and cast the end down to Rafe. He caught it easily.

"Papa first," Kathryn said to Rafe. He shrugged, not caring who went first, as long as they all got up.

"Hold onto the rope, old man," Rafe said through clenched teeth. He tied the line around the man's waist, and Thomas clutched at it. Jack and Wilam heaved him up, but Wilam had to stop to fend off a couple off the pirates who came at them. Jack cast the rope back to the young people on the ship below.

With Thomas over the edge, Rafe turned to Kathryn with the rope in hand. A convulsion shook the vessel as a wave, this one bigger than the last, gushed over. The ship shifted and groaned. All of a sudden, Rafe cried out,

"Wrap the rope around yourself, quickly. Now!" She did as she was told and clutched at it. The ship gave one last groan and began to fall away. Rafe wrapped his arms around Kathryn, one hand holding the rope, when the wooden craft sank away from their feet. Dangling from the end of the slippery cable, both young people shook from terror and looked down at the water raging below them. Feeling them being pulled up to the black galleon, Rafe looked at Kathryn.

"Where did you come from?" Kathryn asked him. "What ship were you on?"

"The captain John Halkins," Rafe muttered. Kathryn looked down at the water once more. "Hey…"

"What?" Kathryn asked, glancing at him.

"I'm sorry…about how I acted on the island," he said softly. She glanced at him. He was looking intently at her. His eyes begged forgiveness. Right then, Kathryn's heart flooded with mercy.

"I do…I do forgive you, Rafe."

It was all Kathryn could do to keep from bursting into tears at the sight of the relief on Rafe's face.

Suddenly, the rope jerked.

"Wilam! Jack!" Kathryn shouted, turning her face up to the rain. Thankfully, the downpour had let up some, and she could see better.

No answer.

"Will! Jack!" Rafe shouted too, growing worried. Finally, the rope was pulled up enough so he could grab the railing. His hands slipped until he found a good grip, then he swung his leg over onto the deck and immediately reached out to help Kathryn. She clutched his wrists, and he hers while he heaved her over the side. As soon as she was on the deck, she looked up and gasped. Rafe turned too, his heart dropping.

Wilam was tied, back to the mast, yelling to them.

"Behind you! Behind you!"

Rafe began to turn his head when he suddenly screamed and fell to the deck, a knife jutting out of the middle of his back. Kathryn gave a sharp cry and backed up a step…right into the arms of the Admiral.

Chapter Fifty

She didn't see her father. She didn't see Jack. They weren't on the deck. She saw Wilam. Wilam. And Rafe…lying on the deck before her, blood spreading out on the back of his shirt.

An arm, burly and muscular, wrapped around her body even tighter. She twisted and tugged, trying to escape…but the grip was like iron. A blade touched her neck. Cold. Sharp. She stopped struggling. She flinched away, her head leaning into the Admiral's chest. The blade pressed harder against her throat.

"So," the voice whispered in her ear. "It comes to this."

"Uncle! Let her go, please!" Wilam begged.

"Silence!" Stepping over the body of Rafe, the fierce arms jerked Kathryn forward until they were not three steps away from Wilam. She could see the hot tears in Wilam's eyes. "You not only refuse to kill this girl, but you also destroy my fleet. All of it! My plan! Everything, you took away from me!" the Admiral was screaming at his nephew. His arms were tensed, tightening his grip on the girl and on the knife. She fought to breathe. He took a deep breath, regaining his composure, and then spat in the boy's face.

"All because of her," the Admiral said quietly. Kathryn whimpered as the blade drew itself across her skin. A drop of blood ran down her throat. "Your allegiance was torn between a girl, and me!"

"No." Wilam growled, "I never felt any loyalty for you. Never! My loyalties were with *my* ship, *my* crew...and Kathryn. Not for you."

"I see..." the Admiral wrapped his arm around Kathryn and stepped towards Wilam, the hand with the knife rose up as he approached the boy. "So now, you die."

A flash of lightning.

A flash of the blade.

"No!" Kathryn screamed as the man thrust the knife in the side of his nephew. A guttural cry wrenched from Wilam's throat. Kathryn was sobbing. He hung at a crooked angle with his hands still bound to the mast, gasping. Blood flowed from the wound as the knife was ripped out.

“Now you can both watch the other die a slow and bloody death…” the Admiral sliced the ropes that bound Wilam’s wrists with the knife that dripped Wilam’s blood and the boy collapsed to his knees on the deck.

Another pained sob escaped between Kathryn’s lips.

Wilam tilted his head up to look at her. Pain was etched into his face as he clutched his side. He was weeping, and not all because of the pain.

“Yes…” the Admiral purred, “Look up here, and watch her die,”

“No!” Wilam cried, terror screaming in his voice. “No, please! I'll do anything. Anything! Just don’t kill her,”

The Admiral ignored Wilam’s desperate cry. He entwined his cold fingers in Kathryn’s hair. She cried out as he jerked her head back, the blade drawing back to pierce her exposed throat. She opened her eyes, tears flowing, and then drew in her breath sharply. Up on the mast, Jack was lowering a rope, a loop tied on the end. A noose.

It came not more than a handbreadth above the head of the Admiral. She stared. What was Jack trying to do? He saw her watching, and placed one of his complete fingers over his lips, telling her to be quiet.

A dark shadow of a ship cast over the deck, causing the Admiral to look up at it. It was the old *Farrow*, her black hull looming over the scene.

"What…what…?" the Admiral murmured, gazing at the vessel. Kathryn saw her chance and slapped the knife out of his hand. It flew into the rescinding waves. The Admiral looked down at her, vehemence igniting in his grey eyes. He wrapped his hands around her neck and constricted his fingers into her flesh, strangling her. Her sight began to dim as she struggled to draw in a breath. She fell to her knees, gripping his wrists with no avail. Her green eyes pleaded silently with the Admiral.

She was fading.

"No!" Wilam cried, and then stood shakily, anger strengthening his body. Blood dripped from his side. He stood, stumbled, and then regained his footing. He gave a cry as he then rushed at the Admiral. The Admiral turned to Wilam, fire in his eyes. He dropped Kathryn. She fell limp, coughed violently, and then collapsed to the deck. Wilam tackled his uncle to the ground. The Admiral winced when his head hit the wood. His eyes lit up again, and he pulled out a knife from in his boot. Wilam rolled off, narrowly dodging the stab. He stumbled. The Admiral was about to advance towards his nephew, but then grinned. He turned to Kathryn, who lay gasping on the deck. He raised the knife. Wilam ran behind the man, pain searing up his side, and pulled at the rope noose. He threw it around the Admiral's neck. By then, the Admiral had clenched the knife above the girl. In desperation, Wilam threw himself on top of her limp body and braced himself for the blow. A roar exploded from the Admiral's throat when the rope jerked up. The knife slipped from his hand and plummeted down towards Wilam. Wilam grabbed it. He stood up and then faced his uncle, who was clawing at the rope furiously. The knife was in Wilam's hand. He raised it. As he advanced towards his uncle, the helpless Admiral in his rage planted his foot in the middle of Wilam's chest. He thrust violently as he was hoisted into the air; Wilam stumbled, unstable, and his arms flailed. Then, he toppled over the edge and fell into the waves.

Jack jerked up on the rope and a snap was heard from the neck when the Admiral's body was hoisted into the air.

"Wilam!" Kathryn screamed, crawling to the railing. "Wilam!"

The water that tumbled around Wilam was cold. He didn't know what way was up. Searing pain knifed up his side. Down, down, down he drifted, no strength in his tired limbs. Something hit him. A piece of wreckage. All he wanted to do was sleep. He didn't care anymore.

He sucked for a breath.

Nothing.

Nothing.

He was still.

He was silent.

Blackness.

She didn't see him. Someone pushed by her and dove into the water.

Moments passed.

Years passed.

As several men helped to drag Halkins and the boy to the deck of the Admiral, Kathryn crouched over Wilam's still, motionless body. Weeping, she took up his head and leaned towards his still face. Brushing the wet curls out of his eyes, she clutched his cold hands in hers. Trembling fingers entwined around his. Her hot tears spilled over his cheeks.

"No, no, no. Wilam," she whispered. *Come back to me. Come back. Wilam. I need you. No. Come back to me.* "God," she found herself praying as she choked on her sobs. "Bring him back to me. He doesn't know Your light yet. Let him see Your light, let him feel it. Let him live. Please God, hear me. Bring Wilam back to me."

She was suddenly aware of his fingers gripping hers lightly. His eyes remained closed. She placed her free hand on his chest, and then broke into tears. A heartbeat. Her tears were of joy when she felt his shuddering, shaking breathing.

"Thank you, God." She whispered. She bent and kissed Wilam's cold forehead and smiled. God had answered her prayer. She was sure now that He was light. He was *her* light. And He was real.

Thunder rumbled in the distance.

Silently Kathryn followed Halkins over to the black *Farrow*, Wilam in Halkins's arms. Some people carried over the bodies from the black galleon, including Rafe's. Several sailors sent the black galleon adrift as soon as everyone was off of its decks.

The sky was dark with the night, but the clouds were beginning to break away. A curtain of stars was revealed as a lonely, silver moon gazed down at her reflection in the calming, ocean waves. The reflection was rippled by the waves carrying away the mutilated galleon with its single corpse swinging from high up on the mast.

The black *Farrow* rested silently, surrounded by several other black vessels. Wreckage drifted by from remains of other vessels. The ocean was hushed, mourning the losses that were wrought from that night. The ship furrowed her black sails and sailed into a calm night, towards the dark shape of the island on the horizon.

Epilogue

John Halkins wrapped the bandage around the wound in Wilam's side, bringing the cloth all the way around his waist. Wilam winced when the old captain pulled it tight. The man grunted, and then cut the bandage.

"Should do it," he said.

"Thank you sir," Wilam said. He ran his fingers through his sandy brown curls and shrugged his shirt on. He didn't bother to button it. "How are all the others?"

The sunlight filtered into the small room, casting a warm glow on the simple furniture, including the bed that Wilam was sitting on. He looked at Halkins earnestly.

"Eh…" the old captain frowned slightly. "You want the good news or the bad first?"

"Uh, good," Wilam hesitated.

"Good news is that Miss Thatcher is alive, with minor bruises on her throat. Jack Cadet survived but lost two of his fingers. The father, Thomas Thatcher, is severely malnourished and weak, but I think he will live. They are all being taken care of in the other clinics. Kathryn really wants to see you." He chuckled.

"The bad news?"

"The boy Rafe Norrington died this morning from blood loss and injuries."

"Oh," Wilam was struck. Although he had felt that he hated the boy, the fact that he was actually *dead* shocked him.

"Of course, we had other losses from the ships: men who were swept overboard, men who died firing the cannons, and the like. Life will go on."

"Where is Kathryn?" asked Wilam.

"She refused to leave your side for most of the night. Just before you woke up, I sent her away so she could rest and I could bandage you."

John Halkins stepped towards the door and opened it.

"Captain?" Halkins turned to Wilam.

"Aye?"

"What will happen now? What do we do, now that the Admiral is gone?"

The man laughed.

"That, my boy, is something you need to decide for yourself. You are now a man. A man with a fresh start and a bright future. Find your place in the world, and make a difference."

The door swung shut, and the captain was gone. Wilam rose, careful of his injured side, and stepped out of the small room. He went down a hall and stepped out of the front door. A cool breeze washed over him, and he took a deep breath of the island. He looked down at the island metropolis below him. No more did the evil flags fly from the rooftops, reminding him of his tattoo. It didn't matter anymore, he thought to himself.

He heard voices. Behind him, he saw Kathryn walking with Meg and Claire. He stopped, waiting for them in the shadow of a palm tree. Meg's pretty face showed traces of tears. Perhaps she was mourning her half-brother. A smile broke over her when Claire said something. The girls laughed.

The youngest girl spotted Wilam and pointed. Kathryn's face lit up when she saw him.

"May I join you?" he asked, bowing to them. All three girls nodded eagerly, and he stepped in line with them. They talked together a little bit as they wandered down the paths, soon well into the forest. Wilam lifted up Claire so she could grab a mango for each of them from one of the trees. As they ate on their little walk, Claire slipped her little hand into Wilam's rough, calloused one. Kathryn and Meg giggled as Wilam looked at them for help when sticky, sweet mango juice dripped from Claire's hand and onto Wilam's. He smiled.

As the sun began to set over the water, the four figures sat on a rocky cliff above the sea, their feet dangling. Meg held Claire, who had fallen asleep on her lap. Kathryn leaned against Wilam, her head on his shoulder, and slipped her hand into his.

"Wilam?" she whispered.

"Mmm?"

"I'm glad you didn't die. Do you want to know why?"

"Why?" Wilam asked.

"So I can show you the light that brought you back to me." she said. He looked at her.

"Yes…" he whispered after a moment and then bent to kiss her forehead. They sat in silence as the sun dipped lower in the sky. As soon as it finally sank beneath the sea, the stars peeked out their diamond heads.

The moon was bright. The sea was calm. The island was silent.

The End

Acknowledgements

First off, all glory and thanks go to my Lord and Savior, Jesus Christ for giving me the chance to share my love of writing and art. Thank you Jesus!

My love and thanks to my first supporter, my first editor, my best friend, and my cousin for all she has done for me and all she means to me, Danielle.

A big thanks to my wonderful, amazing, sweet cousin Kaylyn for all her hard work and endless support and for always keeping me in check.

Thank you to Mom and Dad for loving me and for standing by my side whenever I need you. Thank you for your encouragement in all the things I strive to accomplish.

I am so thankful for the amazing people who sacrificed their time to edit my book and to encourage me the whole time I wrote it. Thank you to Brandon, Mimi, Aunt Lisa, Cody, and Lance.

Finally, I want to thank all the people at my church, my school, and all my friends who were excited and encouraging when I was about to get it published. Thank you so much for always believing in me!

I love you all!

About the Author

Brandy Collins was born in Oklahoma in 2000. She has been homeschooled all of her life. She has always had a passion for writing, art, and Jesus, and does all that she can to display all of these qualities in her writing. *Light of the Black Sails* is her first novel; she wrote it when she was fifteen and published it nearly a year and a half later. Brandy has many hobbies that she enjoys when she is not writing, including: painting, art, hiking, laughing, playing with her dog, and making new friends.

Made in the USA
Coppell, TX
27 December 2020

47145709R00157